IT LOOKS LIKE DAD

It Looks Like Dad © Little Ghosts Books

Published by Little Ghosts Books. Visit us at littleghostsbooks.com

First Printing, April 2023.

Second Printing, August 2024

This is a work of fiction. **Any similarity to actual persons, living, dead, undead, or actual events is purely coincidental.**

Cover Designed and illustrated by Lauren Hope.

Edited by Chris Krawczyk & philip rowan

ESBN: 9781738909704

For Cooper

You were there for every word. Thank you.

IT LOOKS LIKE DAD

1

The tide eroded the footprints on the beach. The surf-themed shops and restaurants on the boardwalk allowed a small rim of melting snow on their rooftops. Pressed against their windows, signs proclaimed they were 'closed for the season.'

Salt-coarse ears of boardwalk cats tensed back at the sound of sand scraping under metal treads. The felines scattered once the harsh yellow light from a truck hit their fur. A teenage boy in a sizeable, goose-down coat with the hood up, sat behind the wheel. His focus wavered on the beach as he listened to an audiobook read by a thin and fragile voice.

"...the people faded away, the arches, the vaulted roof vanished..."

The teenager turned the wheel and, when the headlights passed the ocean, he hit the brakes. Curious about what he thought he might have seen, he looked into the darkness. He put the truck in reverse and redirected the headlights back toward the ocean.

"...I raised my seared eyes to the faithless glare; and I saw the black star hanging in the heavens..."

The headlights reflected something metallic. It was a brief flicker, but it was vibrant. Then the whole of it returned, emerging from the ocean current.

"...and the wet winds from the Lake of Halo chilled my face..."

A bulky silhouette trudged its way out of the oil-dark waters. A coarse, black hose was attached to the back of the figure that led out into the ocean's depths.

It appeared to be an atmospheric diving suit engineered by 19th-century minds. Its sizeable, domed helmet housed a dozen small, glass viewing ports secured with welded bolts. Tubes and cables coiled around the large frame and interlocked at each jagged and barnacle encrusted joint.

Once the majority of its body rose from the water, the weight of the suit crushed the wearer. Each step was labored as it lurched to the shore. A wave crashed against its back, tumbling the diver to its hands and knees. The figure crawled its way to the sand. It got to its knees and unlatched the helmet. A clear, thick sludge poured out from the inside.

A man was found under the metal, vomiting the sludge out of his lungs. With jagged rune tattoos across the bridge of his nose, short hair with bald slits of scar tissue, and a patchy five o'clock shadow, this man inhaled deeply. His lungs gurgled as they remembered how to breathe air. He coughed as he struggled to find a rhythm to his breath, dispelling the last of the sludge.

Once his lungs steadied, he unscrewed some of the cables from his diving suit and tore them away. Swamp-green steam sprayed from the coils and dissipated into the night sky. In a fit of panic, he growled and screeched as he struggled with shaky hands at the latch at the nape of his neck. The front of the hulking suit disengaged from the spine and collapsed into the sand in a metallic heap. The naked and sinewy man then climbed out of his suit. With one foot on the ground, his second lost balance. He collapsed into the sand only to be met with an icy tide.

His scar-riddled body, surgical in nature, convulsed at his freedom. With a steely Frankenstien's monster visage, he looked to have been dissected and reassembled numerous times over. He moaned as he inhaled cold, moist air. With exhausted muscles, he got to his feet and surveyed his surroundings. Seeing the boardwalk, he looked to the sky. The moon was waning, and he reached up to it with an open hand. Awe fermented his psyche and a tortured innocence swallowed his eyes. He closed his fist to cover the moon's glow and hollered triumphantly at the celestial body.

Inside the surfraker, the teenager looked on in confusion. He wiped away the moisture from the windshield, and then his bewilderment dashed to fright. He didn't see him move, but the naked man was looking at him from the hood of the truck.

There were many efficient ways to break into the closed boardwalk diner, and roof access was not one of them. The lack of a stairwell or ladder was the first hurdle, but the man from the sea did not require their aid. The second was fitting a body through the rooftop ventilation. That impossible anatomical feat was also not an issue.

Drywall crumbled from the ceiling, and the shadowed man quickly followed. In the teenager's coat and pants, the man that emerged from the ocean found a light switch. He scoured the diner and found an array of pies and cakes in a glass refrigerator behind the counter. The feeling of glass on his hand churned long-forgotten sensations. He inhaled a gulp of air devoid of putrid moisture and, with genuine euphoria, opened the pie case.

Two police cruisers pulled up to the diner, and four policemen approached the restaurant. Seated at the diner counter, the ocean man sat in front of two empty pie trays, with a third being chipped away. With a solemn expression, he looked over to the flashing lights of the police vehicles.

—

Kaitlin sat in front of a woman caked in neglect. With sun-bronzed skin and experience thinned denim, her shoulders slumped so far forward it looked painful just to exist. Her squeaky office chair kept her focus short.

"I don't know. And I don't want to know," the disheveled Janice told the middle space.

Next to the middle space, Kaitlin sat behind a paperwork-blanketed coffee table. "Why wouldn't you want to know?"

"They don't do nothing for me."

"Not even when you were-"

"No. Never have." Janice interrupted, making eye contact.

"I'm still sure they'd want to know where you are." Kaitlin was legitimately concerned for Janice's well-being, but it took effort. She was afraid the faint exhaustion in her timbre was a signal flare to apathy.

"Don't matter."

"I have to send you somewhere, Janice."

"Still don't matter. Don't care," Janice said, looking back to her nothing.

"You've wandered out of group homes, and you can't just stay at the hospital. "

"I know."

"Then where are we taking you?"

"Drop me off at a Starbucks or something like that. That bread place?"

"Do you really want me to call you a cab to transport you to a Panera bread, just so you can sleep in a public park when they kick you out? Or should we take this opportunity to try and contact your grandchildren to see if you can, at least, get to sleep indoors tonight?" Kaitlin uncapped her blue sharpie as a show of concern. As if with one permanent signature, Janice could sleep in a bed.

"..."

Janice's sincere response was a lack of one. Feeling Kaitlin's eyes, Janice shrugged flippantly at Kaitlin's proposal to end this interaction.

There can be a sense of accomplishment with failure. Having a client feel shame over their own neglect can harbor self-awareness. That acknowledgment could, sometimes, yield better decisions in the future. This was not one of those examples. The worst thing that could happen was being considered an obstacle; a hurdle toward neglect.

After today, Janice wouldn't even consider suicide worth the effort. Kaitlin may have heard about her eventual death, but she wouldn't see Janice again. If Janice learned anything today, it was how to avoid social workers. The cap went back on the Sharpie.

It only took Kaitlin five years to hate her house. It wasn't an overnight realization, but a gradual swelling of animosity. Her commute was where it started. Her schedule was synced with the majority of her neighbors, so she would drive by a safari of groceries being removed from trunks and ties being loosened from necks. Kaitlin originally held disdain for the homes furthest away from her own. 'Who are these people? They look miserable' Kaitlin used to think. That thought crept closer, house by house, until it eventually reached her own.

What was once a lifetime ambition, achieved before her forties, was now a prison at forty-two.

Her two-story townhouse was as white as the first time she stepped inside. Kaitlin saw it as a viewing house, and it never transcended that soullessness. Age brought experience, and experience brought character, but this house refused to age. It denied sentimentality. Kaitlin slept in a synthetic copy of a copy. Therefore, it could never be a home.

Kaitlin pulled into her copy's driveway.

"Noticed your oil leak, there," mentioned the retired Mark in his third polo-shirt-tucked-into-khakis of the day.

"Oh yeah, I got to get on that."

"It's just that, you know, hate seeing it stain the driveway."

"I know. I'm sorry. I just need a free minute to get to it," Kaitlin said as she slung her bag over her shoulder.

"Just hate to see the Community Council crack down on you, if they see it?"

"Why would they care?"

"Some just find it unsightly."

"You find it unsightly?"

"No, no…you know, other neighbors."

"Ah," Kaitlin responded at her door. This could be it. This could be the end of the conversation, Kaitlin thought.

"So, find some time," Mark said with a faux camaraderie.

"I'll see what I can do with my driveway this weekend." *So close.*

"Eeew sooner may be bett-" Kaitlin pretended not to hear the rest of Mark's sentence and entered her house.

Contemplating drinking wine before dinner, Kaitlin grabbed an eight-ounce glass. As she did so, her eyes found a hatchet in the kitchen sink. Mud caked the blade, and dirt-brown water stagnated above a clogged sink. Instead, she filled the glass with water and knocked it back before heading to the back door.

A recent ambition taken upon Kaitlin's thirteen-year-old daughter was the environment. Despite the dwindling autumn, Camilla found it to be the appropriate time to build a garden. To do so, she dismantled the backyard flower bed. Using uneven planks of wood to supply the walls, Camilla filled the garden with escalated soil from nearby plants.

"Cammy, what are you doing?"

"Hey, Mom," Camilla responded without looking at her mother.

"Hey. What are you doing?"

"What's it look like? Getting a garden ready."

"But the flower bed?"

"Eh, rather have food than flowers, right? Plus, I think kale's prettier than something superficial."

"But my flowers. I just thought we would have talked about-"

"We did, remember? I was talking about a garden."

"I was thinking like a tomato plant on the windowsill– didn't you have practice tonight?"

"I'm done with it."

"Done with what? Field hockey?"

"Sports as a whole."

"You talk to dad about all this?"

"I haven't talked to dad for like a month."

"Hm, same. I think he's back tomorrow. Try to make it look like this is supposed to be here," Kaitlin sighed.

"Okay, sure. Whatever that means."

"Just don't need neighbors ratting on us."

"Ah."

"And clean up the sink."

"Will do," Camilla huffed as she dusted off her hands of soil. There was a reasonable instinct to be angry, but exhaustion bludgeoned that compulsion.

Outside the shower, Kaitlin stood naked in front of the bathroom mirror. She had long forgiven her body for rebelling against her wishes, but her immediate concern was her eyes. They appeared to descend further into her skull over the years. It was something other than exhaustion or stress. The darkness under her eyes spread down to her cheekbones.

A long fear of Kaitlin's started to manifest. She was worried that her withdrawn constitution would eventually materialize on her face; as if the malaise would become strong enough to earn tangibility. She was starting to look dead.

Kaitlin laid across the bed with her moist towel acting as a blanket. Even though the sun wasn't yet under the horizon, she contemplated staying in bed.

I could just waste time on my phone until I fell asleep, she thought. *Camilla could feed herself. I'm not that hungry. This is fine.*

Kaitlin found herself sleeping more than she used to. Unfortunately, this was not due to tiredness, but the preference of not existing.

Her phone rang.

"Kaitlin Chambers," Kaitlin answered, "Yes... I don't see how that's possible. He's been in London since January... Business...What do you mean his prints match?... Where did you find him?... And it's him? You're sure?... And he was just... Okay... Okay...Well, if he knew our number... How much?... Does a police station take American Express?"

After hanging up, she called her husband's number. It went to voicemail. "Well, I guess I'm picking you up at the police station. See you in a minute."

Dressed in sweatpants and a button-down long-sleeve shirt, Kaitlin contemplated telling Camilla before leaving. Seeing her daughter sit quietly on a block of wood that used to be a wall to her flower bed was the deciding variable. She didn't even leave a note. The lack of a car in the driveway would be her note.

She requested four-hundred and sixty dollars from an ATM in a vacant convenience store. Four-fifty to release her husband and ten dollars for a bag of salt and vinegar chips instead of a pack of cigarettes.

2

"No charges were pressed, so you should be good to go," a fresh-faced police officer told Kaitlin.

"Thank you," Kaitlin responded as she sat on a bench in the hallway of the police station.

"I'll go get him," the officer said as he walked away.

Kaitlin waited with her smartphone in hand. She checked the time to see that her potato chip fingers left a grease residue on her phone. She used the bottom of her flannel shirt to wipe away when her husband's face appeared on her phone. 'Robert' the phone read with a pudgy, smiling face. She surveyed her surroundings before answering.

"Robert?"

"Hey, yeah, sorry, I missed your call."

"It's fine. I'm out here waiting for you."

"Where?"

"The hallway waiting room area. Not sure if you went through here."

"What do you mean, you're at the airport? What are you doing at the airport? My car's in their lot. And I won't be back until tomorrow."

"But, um-" Kaitlin's bafflement reached a new peak when she heard the door unlock. Out stepped the police officer and 'Robert.'

"Uh, um, okay. I, uh, sorry. See you tomorrow," Kaitlin rambled into her phone.

"Thanks anyway. Love y-" Robert attempted to say before she hung up the phone.

"Here we are," the officer proclaimed as he uncuffed Kaitlin's alleged husband. She reached another peak of bafflement when 'Robert' turned to her.

It was his face. Without a doubt, that was the same skull as her husband, but almost everything else was not familiar. The tattooed, scar-riddled, wiry man that literally crawled out of the ocean was standing in front of Kaitlin. He wore a thin yellow shirt and black dress pants that were bequeathed to him from discarded clothes found in the police locker room.

"You can keep the duds," the officer mentioned as he handed off a printout. "Don't lose your court dates."

The wiry man nestled the papers with a gentle grip between his index finger and thumb. "Thank you, sir," he whispered to the ground.

The officer then left, and Kaitlin looked at the man. The man's eyes stayed on the floor in anxious hesitation. It took him a few tries, but noise eventually left his lips.

"Lin," he said.

"Um, how– ah, how do you know me?" Kaitlin asked as she stood up.

"Rob, I'm Rob. My name's Robert," Rob responded to the linoleum.

"I just talked to my husband."

"London? Am I in London?"

"Uh, yeah. Wait, who are you?"

"Okay…okay," Rob did some mental math as he nodded. "We have time."

"Are you related to Robert? A brother?"

"We're an only child."

"That doesn't make any sense."

"There's an explanation for this."

"Can you look at me?" Kaitlin asked.

"I'm sorry. This is more trying than expected."

"Please."

Kaitlin thought about touching him, but abandoned the thought when she caught a glimpse of the scar that ran across his nose. The man held his breath, nodded, and then looked at Kaitlin. On the verge of hyperventilating, Robert's eyes looked back at her.

At the Wind in Sails Diner (which the limited neon bulbs christened, 'in in ail Din'), Kaitlin sat across from someone she'd been calling Rob. She refrained from eating anything, but Rob ate a full plate of chicken-fried steak with a side of pasta and a baked potato. He was nothing short of polite in asking Kaitlin's permission before ordering. He didn't want to take advantage of the woman who he'd been calling his wife.

"You can pack it in, huh," Kaitlin commented.

"Apologies, my metabolism's probably not what you're used to."

"Hm."

"Thank you, again." Rob felt her eyes on him, but chose to stay focused on his meal.

"No problem. The resemblance is just...it's spooky."

"I understand that."

"I don't."

"I also understand that."

"Listen, you're not my husband. Let's just get that out of the way right now."

"Okay."

"So, you agree?"

"No, I'm your husband."

"Come on, my husband's a stuffy, old, naval architect and you're a patient at the hospital. You saw him and I together, got confused, and assimilated his reality."

"That's what a sane person would think."

"So, it's a possibility?"

"No, I'm a version of your husband. That's a valid assessment for your circumstances, though."

"Eh, come on. I'll go as far as long-lost twin, but that's it."

"Our prints wouldn't match if we were twins."

"But you keep saying "our." As if there could be more than one of the same person?"

"It's going to sound insane."

"How insane?" Kaitlin asked. At this point, she felt she had excavated the enthusiasm from the early days of her social working career.

"Impossible."

"So, like a Soap Opera level of absurd, then. Conjoined evil twins separated at birth?"

"A Doppelgänger, if you will?"

"Exactly."

"I'm more 'Passions' than 'Days of Our Lives.' Except for maybe that exorcism season," Rob regaled.

"The one where Marlena got possessed by the devil?"

"-and Jack Black turned out to be a priest?"

"John. John Black" Kaitlin smirked.

"That's still a ridiculous name. Especially for a priest." Rob chuckled a bit between the sentences. The laugh strongly resembled Robert's, but Kaitlin hadn't heard it for quite some time. Their familiar rapport pinged with her sentimentality, and, for a second, she forgot this wasn't Robert.

"So, you're not a long-lost twin possessed by the devil?" Kaitlin asked after some silence. Rob merely shook his head as the waitress came to their table. With a mellowed apprehension, Kaitlin was open for dessert.

"Can, um, can I get a rice pudding?" Kaitlin asked the waitress.

"Comes with his meal. You want that one?" the waitress dismissed.

"Nah, get an extra one for me. You still want yours?"

Rob's eyes went wide, and he pleasantly shrugged at the proposal.

"Yeah, two rice puddings," Kaitlin responded.

"Sure thing. Whipped cream?" the waitress asked as she bussed Rob's empty plates.

Kaitlin and Rob made eye contact before they nodded in unison. "Yeah, easy sell. Thank you." Kaitlin responded.

"Where were we?" asked Kaitlin, absent from the waitress' ears.

"I'm not a long-lost twin possessed by the devil."

"Oh, good. Clears that up," Kaitlin barbed.

"I'm your husband from a parallel universe's future."

"Oh, Jesus Christ." Kaitlin no longer wanted the rice pudding.

Rob merely gazed outside the passenger's side window of the car. He would gently whimper at specific destinations, but other than the occasional "thank you" or "yes," he remained silent.

For the sixth time since the diner, Kaitlin's phone went to voicemail. She flicked away the audio message before it started to record a message. "Sorry," Kaitlin murmured. "I'll stop trying. That's got to be annoying."

"It's about three in the morning in London, and white noise helped us sleep."

"Rober-uh, sir, just, please. For right now, can we not associate you as Robert."

"I, um…" hearing himself referred to 'sir' shriveled Rob's already tender ego. "Yes. Certainly. Sorry."

"It's okay…" Kaitlin remarked as Rob returned his gaze to the passing neighborhood. "And I don't get it. I know it's still supposed to help you sleep, but white noise is still noise, right? I can't do it."

That deflated ego found some air, and it was a conscious effort for Rob not to smile.

Kaitlin pulled into her house. "Alright, here's the deal. Tomorrow we'll go to the hospital together and find out what to do with you. There's a bathroom in the room out back, so please stay there until I get you in the morning."

"Thank you," Rob's voice cracked. There was a slight pause before 'you.' He did his best to hide his forlornness, but tear pregnant eyes were difficult to conceal.

Rob paused as the two made their way around the back of the house. "The flower bed?"

"Excuse me?" Kaitlin asked.

"It's just, the flower bed…" Rob mentioned looking at a dismantled garden.

"Okay," Kaitlin flippantly mentioned as she made her way to the guest room.

"Forgot she took it apart."

"…what did you just say?" Kaitlin asked after she paused in her stride.

Perceptive to the scrutiny on her face, Rob deflected to, "It's all apart. That's all."

Kaitlin nodded while gripping her keys. Her guest room was more of a shed than a house, but contained just enough furnishment to be considered cozy. A wooden Adirondack chair sat by a desk lamp, and a twin bed raised inches from the floor rested under a tapestry. The tapestry displayed the silhouettes of treetops as a vignette to a bustling cosmos of stars. The fabric was tacked to the ceiling, so the mural's center arched downward toward the bed. A few sun-bleached classics by the likes of Vonnegut and Bradbury were still on the desk, right where Robert and Rob had left them.

"There's a space heater there in the corner if you need it, and the bathroom is that door there," Kaitlin said as Rob shambled his way in.

"Thank you. This is very generous. More than need be," Rob spoke through humbled lips.

Kaitlin's intuition was prodding her to look at Rob's body language. His voice may have been sheepish, but his posture was that of a champion's. His shoulders were back, and his knuckles faced forward. This was when she noticed the symmetry of his scars. Seeing them run across his wrists, arms, and even his fingers, she deduced that they ran across the rest of his body. If that were true, the scarification couldn't have been solely self-inflicted. They were also too clean. Professional. For someone found naked and ostensibly homeless, his body must have cost thousands of dollars. Seeing it in a familiar location boorishly snuffed out any whimsical thoughts that this was actually her husband.

"I'll knock in the morning," Kaitlin said from outside.

"Sure, thank-" Rob said to a closing door.

Left to himself, he remained still until the sounds of the door locking concluded. Then he scoured the room, picking up the book, "Breakfast of Champions" under a stack of others. He flipped right to chapter three. On the blank page before the new chapter, in marker, the words "*Will You Marry Me? - Robert*" were written in cursive. Rob took the book and sat on the edge of the cot. He sighed at the open novel and, as if he were answering an invisible companion, said, "because she loved Vonnegut…Eh, I had faith she'd get through chapter 2."

3

If mornings were a person, Constance would have been arrested for murder decades ago. It was as if she were possessed by a separate human being when her alarm went off. She was content once she was at her desk and the warmth of her coffee mug rested on her thigh. Her brain was then open to information and problem-solving. When her alarm went off, she wished to have died in her sleep. Even in her seventies, she harkened back to when she visited Hawaii as a teenager. She used to love mornings until that trip. There are dew-kissed memories of her being the only one awake in her childhood house. Then, in the act of physiological betrayal, her circadian rhythm tuned into the Polynesian time zone. It just never reacclimatized to Oregon's Pacific Daylight Time zone when she returned.

Today wasn't any different. The alarm went off, and she longed for death. Snooze was hit four times before she eventually sat up. Whoever decided that the universal length of snooze should be nine minutes should be shot, Constance often thought. It's just long enough to fall back to sleep, but short enough to not be restful. Nineteen minutes. It would at least give your unconscious mind the opportunity to prepare for the morning.

At the university, she found the remnants of unfinished research on her desk. Textbooks opened, notebooks were strewn about, and post-it notes peppered most pages. With a plethora of books, but a lack of bookshelf, Constance's collection was merely stacked against the walls. Each stack went about four feet high to where an additional book would topple the fragile integrity of the pile.

She sat behind her desk and turned on her electric kettle, loading her French Press with coffee from a vacuum-sealed bag under her desk.

"Morning, Constance," Roger exclaimed at her doorway.

"Roger, hey. How are you?" Constance responded as she finished her coffee routine.

"Oh, not bad, but…" Roger opened the manilla envelope under his arm. "Four courses, seventy-six students, all 3.O GPA's for the first semester and in the mid-terms of the second."

"It's been a receptive, but not exemplary year," Constance recoiled.

"Maybe convenient's the word."

"Roger, come on."

"If you wanted a sabbatical, you could have asked."

"I always want a sabbatical."

"And that's why you would have been rejected."

"And that's why I didn't ask. Message received, Roger."

"You can't just plug in new numbers. We're interviewing students. Whatever you're working on, save it for the summer."

"It's–" Constance yielded to Roger's insinuation and let a sigh and a nod end the conversation.

"Thank you, Constance. Have a good class." Roger knocked on her door as a half-hearted declaration of gregariousness on his exit.

Constance looked at her open door and then down to her closed book. After a moment of thought, Constance took a discarded notebook from the floor and hurled it toward the door. As the door crept shut, Constance opened her book.

Kaitlin slept unusually soundly. This was one of the rare instances where she didn't fall asleep while the television was on. Better than heroin, she thought of a fulfilling session of slumber. She never actually partook of heroin, dabbled a bit in cocaine, but Kaitlin always assumed the sensation of heroin could not hold a candle to that sinking-into-blankets euphoria of a good night's sleep.

She had time before her alarm, but decided against the extra fourteen minutes of comfort. She wanted to exude a sense of hospitality with a guest on the premises. There were vague memories of making a frittata a few years ago. It wasn't that hard. Eggs and cheese in a baking tin. She could probably do that again.

Under the cot, Rob nestled himself in the fetal position, encased in a chrysalis of blankets, sheets, and pillows. The sound of wood gently clattering tip-toed into Rob's morning. Waking up, the first thing he saw was the grain of the wooden floor. He used the sight to meditatively reverse engineer where he was. He was on top of stained wood that wasn't covered in dust, moist or distressed. Therefore he was in a controlled environment. There must be some form of temperature control which means he's in a place with access to power which means there's a minimal chance of an immediate threat. He's in a safe place, put there by someone he could trust. That's when he recognized he was in the guest room of his wife's home. While he was in upstate New York, there was a semblance of order and civility.

He rolled out from under the cot and got to his feet without using his hands. To awaken, he clasped his hands together and cranked them over his head until he touched his tailbone. As his joints contorted, not a sound was made. For something so visually agonizing, Rob yawned a morning exhale and touched his toes. As he put on his police handout pants, he found where the sound of clattering originated. Through the window, he saw Camilla working on the garden. Rob covered his mouth before a whimper left his throat. Tears swelled over his eyes, and his vision became clouded vignettes. "Cammy," he said with a thin voice. As penance for staring, Camilla didn't hear Rob's whisper, but did find him in her peripherals.

There was a knock at Constance's door. Since it wasn't completely closed, it crept open to Roger's face. Constance heard Roger before she saw him. "Constance. These officers need your assistance."

"Pardon me?" Constance asked.

Behind Roger stood a redwood of a man garbed in a white button-down, brown tactical cargo pants, and a pristine, lambskin, leather jacket. Constance didn't immediately see her, but eclipsed by the man was a slinky woman in a black turtleneck, black jeans, and an earth-tone green trench coat. At the sight of the woman, Constance's back tensed, and her teeth gritted. "Roger, please leave."

"Let me facilitate-" Roger stammered.

"Roger, now. Please."

"You're all good, sir. You got us where we need to be," the man chirped as he made his way into Constance's office. The woman followed, and Constance made some distance between her and her desk. She primed her body for conflict as she positioned her weight over her hands, clutching the armrests of her chair, and pressed the balls of her feet onto the floor. The woman closed the door behind her.

" 'lo, Constance," the man said a few feet away from her desk.

"Leonard."

"It's been a tick, apparently."

"It has been some time, yes," Constance responded.

"Thirty years-ish?" Leonard asked.

"Thirty-two."

"Stress accelerates cellular degeneration," the woman remarked as she retrieved a cigarette as black as pitch from a bronze case.

"You can't smoke in here."

"You know it won't," the woman responded as she twisted the end of the cigarette. She then inhaled the slender cylinder, and the tips glowed a gentle electric hue. Upon her exhale, her lips and cheeks faintly housed the current, revealing a glimpse of her teeth through the bellow of skin.

"Miss those?" Leonard asked Constance.

"I suppose I wouldn't be able to bum one?"

"Eh, why waste one?"

≈

"Mom! You in the house-" Camilla shrieked up the stairs as she did the same.

"What? Yeah? You okay?" Kaitlin responded while sliding her blue sharpie into her front pocket.

"I called the police. There's someone in our backyard. In the shed!"

"Oh shit, when?"

"I don't know, a minute ago?"

"Shit, Cammy. He was with me."

"What?"

"He's a patient."

"Why didn't you say anything?"

"Did he do anything?"

"Crying and screaming."

"Crying and screaming?"

Outside, all that was left of Rob was a bundle of blankets. Kaitlin opened the locked door from the outside, so it was alarming that he could have left the shed at any time. The window that was ten feet in the air may have room for the slender Rob, but he would've had to remove the entire pane to do so.

"Put down the shovel. He flew the coop," Kaitlin alerted her coiled spring of a daughter.

"But he's gone, right?"

"Yeah, guess you scared him off."

"But he's gone?"

"Yes."

"Thought you locked the door?"

"So did I. Oh, what a treat; let's go talk to some police?" Kaitlin mumbled when she saw the flickering red and blue reflection against the neighbor's house.

"You had a big 'ol chunk o' time. Find anythin' enlightening? Expand your vocabulary?" Leonard asked the stiffened Constance.

"Get to know your younger self?" The woman asked. Constance sneered at her for that question.

"No."

"Thought that was your lineage's vocation in life?"

"It ends with me."

"It astounds me how much I don't believe that."

"So, what've you been up to?" Leonard asked.

"It's been an on-and-off-again relationship between reaffirmation and substance abuse."

"Considering everything, and literally everything, if there were another result, wouldn't someone else have figured it out by now?"

"That's the reaffirmation part."

"And where's that leave you?"

"And that's the substance abuse part."

"You can still swear allegiance. Thirty years is not even a breath in their lives," the woman mentioned as she finished her electric cigarette.

"If it's that infinitesimal, why bug an old drunk?" Constance responded.

"Loyalty's rewarded."

"In more ways than one," Leonard added.

"If you consider being a well-fed slave a 'reward'?"

"Slaves don't have a choice. We did."

"Yeah? What alternatives did you have? What other choices did you turn down?" Constance asked. After a stale moment of silence, Leonard smirked while the woman scowled. "I guess you're looking at it."

"Well, for what it's worth, ya certainly narrowed down our options," Leonard chuckled.

"So, there's no sign of a forced…exit?" a rotund state police officer asked. The bulletproof vest couldn't conceal his swollen gut, but it did mask his shoulders. Jagged and bulky, his girth was accompanied by strength.

"To a location, he was invited to?" a short and hairless officer added as he jotted down notes.

"I know. It's just that my daughter called you guys and was unaware that he was a patient," Kaitlin responded, standing in her empty shed.

"Is it a permissible action for a social worker?" asked the stout officer.

"Pardon me?"

"Taking your work home with you," the officer sneered.

"In extreme circumstances, yes," Kaitlin lied.

"Alright, then."

"So, you allowed a client to stay on your property, and you don't know his name?" asked the sturdy officer. The men sat on stools by the kitchen island while Kaitlin made coffee. Camilla sulked by the fridge.

"He was on a waiting list at the hospital, and I couldn't get to him, so I let him sleep in the shed. We were going to review his case first thing in the morning," Kaitlin informed the officers, but spoke to the coffee grounds.

"So, was it the tattoos or scars that compelled you to let a parolee onto your property?" the bald man asked.

"Excuse me?" Kaitlin slithered.

"Or both? I'm just curious what it was about this man that led to your hospitality," he asked as he nodded to his partner. As Kaitlin pondered a lie, she became alert to the sight of the hefty officer inserting a rust-colored sliver of metal into his radio receiver. It was quick, but she may have made out a glimpse of an etching. It reminded her of the symbols riddled on Rob's body. She then wondered why these were state police as opposed to local police.

"Mike Bravo 471 to BKE," the officer said into his receiver.

≈

"Mike Bravo 471 to BKE," the woman's receiver blurted on her belt.

Constance used the distraction as an opportunity and hurled her desktop into the air. The top of her custom wooden desk was attached to the base with hinges, and once it was hoisted into the air, it locked into a vertical position. As papers, books, and pencils occupied the air, Leonard thrust his chest toward the wooden pane. With a snap that resembled a whip crack, the desk splintered in half.

"Shit." Leonard said at the sight of an absent Constance.

"10-6 MB 471," the woman spoke into her receiver. The two then rounded the desk to scour the area for Constance.

Leonard's shirt was opened, and his buttons weren't buttons at all, but magnetic studs that kept his shirt closed. A loose paperclip was magnetized to his shirt. He flicked off.

"Well, there you go," Leonard exclaimed as the woman hoisted the wooden halves together. "Looks like she did expand her vocabulary." Glyphs were painted under the desk, and once the top of the desk was raised, it made one complete sigil. "What do you think? Pursue?"

The woman shook her head. "She had time to prepare. Even if it worked after some assembly, it'd be a trap."

"Yeah?"

"It's what I would do."

"Ah," Leonard shrugged.

The woman returned to her radio. "10-8 471."

"10-61, no sign of priority 2," the receiver crackled.

"Who's there, 471?"

"W and D."

The woman looked at Leonard. "Kaitlin spent more time with him?"

"Hey, if you're cool with it, I'm cool with it, Cici," Leonard chirped.

"26 W, 86 D," Cici reported into her radio.

"Copy, BKE," the officer said to his receiver.

The muscular officer retrieved his taser when Kaitlin clinked two coffee mugs onto her kitchen island. Like a dead tree, Kaitlin went down with stiff legs. Her head met linoleum right before a 'thank you' was motioned by the assaulting officer.

Catatonic at the sight, Camilla looked at the squat officer pointing his taser gun toward her. "Wait, I'm-" and much like her mother, she also went to the floor. Camilla landed face down. The only thing within the purview of Kaitlin's paralyzed vision was her daughter's ankles.

It was such an unceremonious and harsh realization to know tears could operate after being tased, but not a voice. Her silent consciousness roared in motherly horror even as nothing escaped her mouth. Kaitlin pleaded with her body to reciprocate, but it only produced a gentle coo. She watched as the short officer flipped over Camilla's body and unholstered his sidearm. He retrieved a silencer from a pouch in his vest and screwed it onto the barrel of his weapon. Kaitlin's eyes went wide. *At least let me die before it happens,* she thought. She didn't.

He fired two bullets into Camilla's chest with the blasé demeanor of performing household chores. The pop of the muffled gun was still loud enough to ring Kaitlin's ears. Instead of screaming, Kaitlin's jaw contoured in ways that ignited an agony-laden spasm in the meat of her jaw. She silently begged to die.

As the officer moved the trajectory of his gun from Camilla's chest to her forehead, a naked Rob shattered his way through the kitchen window. He clasped onto the gun-wielding hand and wrenched it until the bones in the officer's wrist snapped apart.

The hulking officer went for his handgun, but was subdued before his fingers could touch the handle. From the small of his back, up his spine, and ending at Rob's shoulder blades, a separate living creature dislodged itself from Rob's torso. Leaving Rob's body a thinner and transparent membrane-covered spine, a two-foot-tall, four-foot-wide, spider-like animal lived inside Rob's body; camouflaged as a human back.

The spindly monstrosity leapt onto the powerful officer. The hooked, black pincers at the ends of its legs dug themselves into the assailant's neck and skull. Mandibles on the creature's face tore through the man's eyes as he attempted to press the monster away, only succeeding in digging the talons deeper.

As for Rob, in the flash it took him to snap the bald cop's arm, he shoved his free hand into the man's agape and screaming mouth. Rob's left hand unlatched between the middle and ring finger, revealing a small, fleshy orifice encased in fine hairs. With his left hand in the policeman's mouth, the slit pulsated to pump venom into the victim's throat. Rob ended the confrontation by grasping onto the man's jaw and yanking his head down to the kitchen floor, shattering the tile upon impact.

One of the two was dying, so Rob turned to the second. "Rudy!!" Rob hollered, and the spider creature sprang off the giant man's face. Rob's right hand also housed artillery.

Loading his strike, two fang-like quills lanced their way through the skin of his wrist, went through his palm, and locked into place on the back of his hand. With all the force his body could call upon, Rob delivered an uppercut to the second assailant. The fangs pierced through the soft tissue under his chin, and all three hundred and eighteen pounds of the man was hoisted into the air. With an arm outreached, Rob kept his foe suspended. Once the bloodied and eyeless face of the man relaxed to death, Rob flung him away.

"Thank you, Rudy," Rob said to the spider. The spider responded with a series of clicking noises. "Please," Rob answered. Rudy the spider then dashed away, and Rob went to Camilla. "Come on, Cammy, I got you. I got you." Rob hoisted Camilla off the ground and laid her across the kitchen table. "I'm sorry, Cammy. I'm sorry."

After regaining the feeling in her appendages, Kaitlin finally found her feet under her. The bald policeman was still alive. His face, the color of eggplant, was swollen enough that his eyes were hidden under a layer of ballooned skin. Mouth agape, Kaitlin unintentionally watched his last guttural exhale.

Perplexed to the brink of fainting, she found a prize worth relinquishing her consciousness. A nude Rob was performing open heart surgery on Camilla. 'Open heart' in that the surgeon's heart was exposed. Rob's left rib cage was splayed open like a gate in a fence. His ribs didn't resemble bone, but crustacean-like legs with interlocking sinew and jagged tendons. And that pumping lump of organs was not his heart, but his stomach. The stomach in his chest was encased in a translucent and moist chassis of bone and veins. Below his billowing intestines and in front of his wheezing lungs several pitcher-shaped sacs pulsed. Gently squeezing one of the sacs with his left hand, Rob dipped his right hand's fangs in the pouch's fluid.

"Please, Cammy, Dad's got you," Rob said as he inserted fangs into Camilla's wound. "There we go, there we go," Rob whispered to himself as he continued to operate. "Heart's still beating, heart's still beating." Rob pressed his lips against hers, tilted her head back, and breathed into her. The fangs remained in her torso. "Bullet," Rob exclaimed as his pincers drew a bullet from her body. "Other went through, so, come on…" Rob breathed into her once more, and Camilla's chest inflated with air. She remained conscious. "Good, good," Rob hushed as he continued to enter her wounds with hormone-laced fangs.

"Our daughter's going to live," Rob said to a mortified Kaitlin. She then looked into the eyes of the monster that resembled her husband. With the majority of his thoracic muscles missing and his ribcage agape, diffused light shined through his mucus-slathered entrails.

"You okay?" Rob attempted to ask a flabbergasted Kaitlin.

Rudy returned, rushing to his host and landing on the kitchen counter. He clacked his mandibles together toward Rob.

"Thank you," Rob said to Rudy. "Our perimeter is clear," Rob assured Kaitlin.

Much like the eyes of a chameleon, Rudy's eyes could operate independently from each other. All eight of them looked at Kaitlin, including the two prominent human eyes.

Once again, her head met linoleum.

-
-
-
-
-
-
-
-

4

In an abandoned mall, Constance stood behind a concrete divider sixty-nine feet away from a graffiti-smattered escalator. The same sigil drawn under her desk was painted on its side. With breath held hostage by her lungs, she gazed at the sigil carved on the damp wall. She held onto an orange hand plunger attached to an egg timer. A nest of wires led out of the kitchen appliance into a metal safe embedded in the concrete floor.

It was dark. Even with the dust-imbued light from a grime-caked skylight, it was dark. This was a concrete swamp and butane lighters were the fireflies. The addicted souls looked on, withdrawn in their moldy shadows. As glimmers of decaying teeth flashed in curdling department stores, Constance stayed vigilant.

Constance felt her diaphragm knot. As her gut asked to exhale, she pressed her tongue against the roof of her mouth. She couldn't go on without passing out. She let go of the lever and then her breath. Even though she exhaled, her agency remained. She cranked the egg timer, placed it into the safe in the ground, and then jogged away "everyone in here, get the fuck out of here!"

In the rotting parking lot, Constance rattled as her homemade bomb detonated. She and some lingering hermits were far enough away to avoid damage. Concrete, dust, and debris shattered through the department store entrance, but the structure remained intact. Even though she briefly stopped in her march, Constance did not turn to look at her work.

Constance only remembered what was in her storage garage when she gripped its handle. *Oh fuck, that's right,* she thought before lifting the door open. The sun illuminated the culprit for her cerebral vulgarity. She was twenty-eight at the time, and a Vespa seemed appropriate for a daring escape. Now in her late sixties, in the thralls of a Northeastern October,

Constance reluctantly hoped it wouldn't start. She intermittently stored away a few thousand dollars inside its caboose, but it had been eleven years since she'd returned for upkeep. She could buy a used four-door junker instead of frigidly fleeing from emerging danger at a top speed of forty-three miles per hour. Then again, her twenty-year-old black market TNT went off without issue.

Up on wooden blocks, Constance re-inflated the deflated tires before rolling the bike onto the ground. She refused to deem this a vehicle. If you were using a fire-engine-red bicycle pump, it was a bike. Vespas used mostly thermoset plastics and aluminum for their bodies. Unfortunately, this 'bike' was purchased right before the transition, so it was primarily made of steel and sheet metal. If it fell over, she couldn't lift it from the ground. Leaning it on the kickstand, she filled the tank with forty-year-old gasoline and reconnected the battery.

"Well..." Constance uttered as the sea-foam green Vespa kicked to life, "...Shame." She sighed as she secured her emergency backpack and supplies to the back of her seat. Wrapped in her tarp, clothes that would no longer fit nestled next to blankets, the anarchist cookbook, and a parka. She zipped herself up inside the coat, put on mittens, and slipped on a wool beanie followed by a pink helmet. She puttered a few feet before she wobbled to a stop.

"Ugh..." Constance groaned into her visor.

Relieved by the lack of cars at Dr. Bumble's Diner, Constance drifted to a stop. Years of neglect allowed the painted lines on the concrete to fade into the ghost of a parking space. The red neon was still lit 'Open,' but the overgrowth of adjacent branches swallowed most of the diner. The sun-bleached, front-facing windows and doorway were the only things saved from the shrubs, vines, and weeds. This eatery was an unceremonious example of nature's potential for malevolence.

Or the Devil's playground, Constance thought at the sight of the twisted briers warring with coarse vines. She had to step over roots that were protruding through cracked concrete to get to the ramp for the entrance.

An elderly couple sat in a booth, and three road workers sat at the counter. None of them looked at Constance when she walked in. A muted TV projected the news as it sat atop a mini-fridge. She took off her parka as she sat at the counter and was given a cup of coffee without asking.

"Um, thank you," Constance said to a nodding waitress. A chalkboard revealed the menu under a layer of dust. It was the standard breakfast affair, and the last revision was a crossed out 'link' and scribbled in red marker 'patty.' She looked up at the silent waitress. "Uh, pancakes and sausage, I guess," Constance asked.

"Toast?" The waitress responded.

"Brown, if you have it."

"We don't," the waitress said as she walked away.

Constance looked at the TV. It was reporting on a local water main rupture. It was 8:53. *Oh yeah, time zones*, Constance thought at the sight. After some mental math, Constance looked at her waitress. "Excuse me, is it okay if we turn the news off?"

"What channel ya thinking?"

"Just off, if that works?"

"Sure? We got more than news."

"Not for long."

<u>5</u>

"The state, not D.C.?" a police officer asked.

"That's right," Leonard responded.

"So, when did you get in?"

"Literally walked off a plane an hour ago," Leonard said inside the crime scene that used to be Kaitlin's house.

"But when were you called in, 'cause we didn't get wind of this until a neighbor called in around eight? These two didn't even report anything after the nine-one-one call, and that wasn't made until around seven. Dispatch couldn't even find reports of the other two in the back being called in for assistance."

"Most likely due to being murdered," Leonard quipped. Adjacent officers frowned at his disrespect.

"Yes, but when did you specifically-"

"It's similar to a west coast investigation, so we got the call. So, Officer... *Shit-less-*" Leonard intentionally misread from the Detective's badge.

"Shytles," the officer corrected.

"Yes. Shytles. Of course. So, my partner and I are here to comb the premises. If you need anything, please don't be afraid to holler," and with a rough pat on Detective Shytles' shoulder, Leonard walked away from the baffled man.

The officers Rob killed were still on the floor. Police peppered evidence markers throughout the kitchen as they discussed, bypassing the laborious amount of blood. It was a landscape painting of gore. Police in latex gloves and disposable shoe covers scoured every crevice. Without hand or shoe coverings, Leonard stepped over the stout officer's body and stood next to his partner. Trekking in the blood created a delicate ripple through the red. One officer thought the minuscule crest was reminiscent of skipping a stone on a lake. The disgust returned once she realized it had tipped over a paper evidence marker.

Leonard's flagrant disregard for standard crime scene procedure did not go unnoticed. He had a badge, but his demeanor resembled an FBI agent on syndicated television rather than the arid and pedantic automatons that roamed reality. Then again, no officer here had ever seen anything like this.

Cici was standing by the back door, staring at the shed. Police were doing the same with two more bodies of police officers being bagged inside. "Looks like he was hiding those two when we were talking to these two," Cici surmised.

"Cat's out of the bag when you cut down two cops in front of your family," Leonard added. They looked at the bodies on the floor of the kitchen. Swollen for hours, their pillows of skin deflated into a wrinkled heap of leather. The muscular corpse's left leg was removed at the hip and the femur. There were no signs of the missing appendage on the premises. Rob's venom made his victims' blood unable to coagulate, so the red remained a liquid that bathed the entirety of the kitchen floor.

"Well, at least he's fed," Leonard said at the gore.

"And has been on the road for about an hour and a half."

"Unless he used a gate."

"There wouldn't be an efficient one close enough for upstate."

"We sure they're heading that direction?"

"I would," Cici mentioned while staring out at the garden.

"Please, please, please, let me in my home!" Robert cried. Outside the house, Kaitlin's flabby husband pleaded for admittance to his own home. Hurling his briefcase away and loosening his tie for air, Robert involuntarily sat on the grass. A paramedic and Detective Shytles went to his aid.

"Oh my god, please be who I want that to be," Leonard cackled.

"It is," Cici responded.

"Hehehe."

The sunken eyes of Robert looked to Leonard and then to Shyltes. "My family? Is that my family in there?"

—

Kaitlin woke up forty-three minutes ago and spoke only three words since. Rob attempted to ask her if she was okay and, before he could finish the sentence, was met with a frozen, "don't."

Camilla slept in the backseat. When Kaitlin found her, she reached back and asked, "Is she-?" before finding two freshly healed scars in lieu of bullet wounds. Rob attempted to explain that she'd be fine, but he was met with another yet equally frigid, "don't."

Rob silently drove as suburbia gradually transformed into tree-entombed backroads. As the scenery evolved, Kaitlin's eyes gradually wondered about Rob's anatomy. Remembering his disgusting construction of claws and mucus, she speculated on how his body operated. He ate, but how was it digested?

"My eyes are up here," Rob attempted to joke.

"Yeah, where's your heart?" Kaitlin asked.

Rob sighed from the disdain in her voice. "Uh, the way to a man's heart, well hearts," Rob amicably retorted as he motioned to his lower abdomen. "One on each side."

"…that's ridiculous."

"I know."

"Understandable."

"So, where's your stomach?"

"Um, I think you may have gotten a look at it. My poison glands outline my digestive tract, which are behind my ribs." Rob described with a cautious glint. "My pelvis protects my hearts, and the two sets of muscular systems on each side of my endo-skeleton encase my-"

"Stop, just stop."

"I'm sorry. Sorry. I don't get to talk about it much-"

"Please."

"Yes, sorry. Too soon."

After a beat of silence and Kaitlin attempting to find a new place to stare, she yielded to the obvious, "Where are you taking us?"

"Ah, our cabin."

"What? Our 'Our' cabin?"

"It's, um, safer there."

"How do you know about the cabin?"

"I…" even though Rob didn't hesitate to eviscerate four men that morning, he had to find the courage for this conversation. "I'm from a parallel Earth that went through an apocalyptic catastrophe. It's going to happen here, and I wanted to try and keep my family safe from it."

Kaitlin merely stared at Rob as he attempted to keep his eyes on the road while gauging her reaction.

"It's, um-" Rob puttered.

"Can we pull over?"

"Why?"

"I could use some water and a bathroom," Kaitlin blatantly fibbed.

"I don't know if we're far enough north to-"

"I don't know what's going on. Anything I thought I knew about everything is wrong. My life is forever changed, and it all went to shit in less than twenty-four hours. Pull over." Kaitlin hissed through her teeth.

"I just think it's-" Rob's meek rebuttal would wilt away mid-sentence even if Kaitlin didn't interrupt.

"And this is kidnapping."

"…um, sure…sure. We could actually use the gas," Rob appeased.

They turned into an independent gas station. Mounds of mulch outlined the parking lot, and the time-weathered bungalow behind the pumps told its story. In the fifties or sixties someone installed two gasoline pumps in front of their home and didn't do anything else since. A leathery man in faded denim was proof of that. In a ball cap that has spent more time on his head than hair, he sat in his small convenience store shed in front of his pumps. He shuffled out of his shed.

Kaitlin found her shoes on the floor of her seat. She wasn't wearing them at the time of the attack, so Rob must have grabbed them. Rob saw her discovery and mentioned, "I packed what I could. You both have suitcases in the trunk," Rob paused, then added, "Hope that's okay? I-"

"Hi there, bathroom?" Kaitlin asked as she exited the vehicle.

"Around the side," the gas man said as he attended his pumps.

"Thank you." Kaitlin walked off as the gas station attendant took the gas cap off her vehicle.

"What's you need?"

"Fill up, please," Rob responded as he leaned on the car. Rob's eyes look to the sleeping Camilla in the back seat.

"We just missed it," the gas station attendant grumbled.

"Scuse me?" Rob responded.

"The wave. Cuba and the Dominican are gone. Wave hit it. Florida and Venezuela are feeling it too."

Rob sighed at the news and rubbed his scalp in sorrow. He looked past the man and at the flickering box television in his shed. It was a window into the devastation. Cars floated into buildings as rooftop survivors hollered at helicopters. The image came from Miami. The bottom news ticker reported Estimated Casualties in the tens of millions.

"Sorry, that's right. Do you have family there?" Rob asked.

"Nah, been to Cuba as a boy. Y'know, before ya couldn't."

"Ah. Never been."

"And looks like ya won't ever."

"Tragic. World won't be the same."

"World might not be; folks will."

"That supposed to be grim?"

The gas station attendant didn't even attempt to make eye contact despite Rob's attempt. "Peoples are people." The man shrugged as the gas finished with a ding. "And not much more than that."

"Do you have family near here, maybe closer inland?"

"Mh?"

"Family near here?"

"Brother in Chenango."

"You should visit him as soon as you can," Rob suggested with an outreached fold of bills.

The eye contact Rob longed for finally came to fruition. It was immediately followed by a disgruntled head shake and a mumbled half-hearted thought. The man handed Rob roughly the correct amount of change and shimmied back into his shack. Even though the conversation was under two minutes, the gas station attendant preferred a static-filtered catastrophe.

Inside this uncharacteristically clean bathroom, Kaitlin jettisoned the last of her vomit into the sink. Due to dehydration, the drain wouldn't discard the more significant remnants of her salt and vinegar chips.

The further we get out of civilization, the more Rob will reveal his intentions. That could be bad, she thought.

As she wiped away the last of her vomit, she found a spider on the wall. After shoveling the last of her stubborn vomit with a clump of toilet paper, she crushed the spider with it. She then picked up the Sharpie she dropped from nervous hands and exited the bathroom. The bathroom mirror read in blue, 'HELP Kaitlin & Camilla Chambers kidnapped Red SUV B890D37 Call Police Going 1317 GlassLake NY'

Kaitlin stepped out of the bathroom to see her car parked in front of the facility. Rob was leaning against the car with her smartphone in hand.

"You have my daughter. I'm not going to make a break for it," Kaitlin said while approaching the car.

"This is yours," Rob said as he gave Kaitlin back her phone.

"Why would you give this back?"

"First of all, it's yours, second…" Rob walked to the driver's seat. "You should read the news." He left Kaitlin outside of the car, free to roam, with her phone. Like a migraine, possibilities pried their way into her skull. She could call the police. She could get into the car and text the police. She could call friends and family to have them contact the police. As far as she knew, there were two rotting police officers on her kitchen floor. She did miss messages from her work associates, but news alerts dominated her screen.

As Kaitlin scrolled through the horror, the gas station attendant walked into the bathroom and immediately walked back out. Kaitlin leaned on the car as her brain drowned in shock. She had to remember how to breathe. She slinked her way back into the car. Two equally unsettling thoughts raged behind her eyes; *this is awful,* and *does this validate Rob?*

"I don't know what this means."

"I understand," Rob said while holding the steering wheel.

"Don't patronize me on this."

"I understand that it's... difficult to understand."

"I hate you, but please, reassure me. You're not going to hurt us?"

"My whole reason for being here is to keep you- What the hell?!" Rob's changed tone was met with an echoing shotgun blast.

"Alright, fella, step out of the car," the gas station attendant barked as he lowered a smoking barrel.

"Shit! Shit!" Kaitlin hollered as she looked at the approaching gasman.

"Keep an eye on them. I'll engage when the barrel breaks the parallel," Rob whispered loud enough for Kaitlin to hear.

"Wait, are you talking to-" and Rob was gone. With one hand, Rob was able to pull himself through the driver's side window. The gasman couldn't get his bearings before Rob leaped off the car's roof and gripped onto the shotgun's barrel. Not realizing his weapon was out of his hands, he saw his gun being hurled deep into the woods.

"Off me, Fucker!" the man roared as he was pinned to the ground. Rob's knee pressed on the man's sternum as he gripped the car's fender for leverage. Rob didn't strike the leathery attendant, but he was ominously pressing his palm over the man's eye. "Kill you. I'm gunna kill you!"

"No, no, no, no, no, stop, stop! You got him! Stop!" Kaitlin ordered as she stepped out of the car.

"I'm not going to kill him!" Rob responded.

"I'm gunna kill you!" the gas man slurred.

"Sure you are, tiger."

"I'm not yer tiger, ya fuckin' milksop!"

"Not sure how to interpret that."

"I'm sorry, sir. This has gotten out of hand," during Kaitlin's apology, she realized Rob's shirt was in ribbons. His back was once again absent of flesh. "Oh, shit."

Due to the commotion, Camilla stirred awake. The first thing she saw, after being shot, was a seventy-eight pound spider named Rudy.

6

Leonard walked back to his car faster than the traffic on the interstate. Instead of sitting back in the driver's seat, he leisurely leaned up against the passenger's side door. Cici was smoking an electric cigarette as she ashed it from the open window.

"How's it looking?" Cici asked, looking at the gridlock.

"Bumper to bumper as far as I can see," Leonard responded.

"That is bad."

"Don't I know it."

"Out of all the outcomes, this is the most inconvenient."

"Don't know about that."

"We had two responsibilities, and we failed at both."

"Noooo. No. Failure implies we're done. We're not. We're 'failing.' There's a difference."

"Whatever justification keeps you content."

People gave up trying to endure the traffic and started roaming the space between vehicles. Cici's insensate gaze found a family of four holding hands around a makeshift dinner on the hood of their car. As they prayed over their deli meats and white bread, Cici ate the end of her cigarette. Their dinner table was a four-wheel drive SUV, and they were stuck on the outside edge of the freeway. Only the six-year-old girl kept her eyes open during grace.

"Think we could navigate through the woods?" Cici asked.

"On foot? Don't see how with our cargo."

"A few ATVs are using dirt roads. Think it would fit that SUV?"

"You mean the one with the family circus eating engine hot bologna?" Leonard larked.

"Yes."

"That's a naughty thought."

"They have about an hour left anyway."

"You want to gut 'em?"

"I mean, why waste time with badges and explanations? The keys are even on the hood."

"A quick shock and a getaway?"

"I'm willing if you are."

"You want to grab our dude, or should I?"

"You, I don't want to look at him," Cici said as she stepped out of the car.

The father of the group was the first to see a wasp on the sleeve of his jacket. Two inches long, with a flanged black and yellow thorax, it seemingly had more legs than it needed; far more than six, with several accompanying thin, translucent wings. With mandibles visible to the human eye, the father didn't believe he was looking at a wasp on the eve of autumn. When it looked at him, he gasped in primordial terror. He swatted at it and was met with a thin stream of warm liquid. His eyes immediately swelled shut from the acid excretion. Even though his hand met the insect, the creature did not fold. It remained intact and incessantly stung at his wrist. A venomous hole bore back the flesh of the man's skin, and he slunk to the ground in sluggish agony. As the rest of the family saw their father perish, most of them fell to the same fate. Dozens of hell-graven wasps saw to their end, except for one.

Leonard opened the trunk. Handcuffed, Robert looked up at his assailant. "Come on, buddy. Jumping ship," Leonard told Robert as he hoisted him out of the vehicle.

Cici was already in the driver's seat of the SUV when Robert was crammed into the backseat. "Please, please, please, don't hurt me! Whatever you want, don't-" Robert exclaimed.

"Be quiet. Quiet!" Cici responded, and her voice lacerated into Robert's psyche. He'd only ever heard Leonard's. Stunned by the response, he stayed still across the back seat. Leonard ran around to the passenger's side.

"Let's roll," Leonard said as he sat down. Cici put the car into reverse and plowed into the car behind them. Mercilessly creating distance by repeatedly bulldozing her way into the traffic in front of and behind them, Cici found it difficult to find traction on the dead family under their own car.

"Smooth," Leonard slithered through cackling teeth. Once the car was free, the sounds of hollers and shrieks could be heard rather than concussed metal. "Freedom!"

Roberts' body struck the roof as the SUV met the forest. Cici revved through the shrubbery and, eventually, found flat land. The trail was just wide enough for their escape vehicle.

"Woo! Nice road work!"

"Let's see how far we can get before we need to do this again," Cici said as the car rattled onward.

On the freeway, the six-year-old girl remained intact from Cici's assault. Free from wasp sting and vehicular damage, she sat, mortified and drooling at the bodies of her mangled family. Her mind surrendered to horror. She couldn't even hear the roar of the civil defense siren.

—

It was faint and distant, but it was enough to stop Constance in her ascent. It bellowed in the cacophony of wind and labored breathing, but it was there. Constance held her breath. A siren. From all directions.

"Shit," Constance uttered as she continued up the steps. Her legs started to cease, and seemingly in-between steps, she felt as if she was wading through tar.

The combination of height and exhaustion nipped at Constance's dread. Never one to be afraid of heights, the trudge, assisted by the circumstances, molded into one. It was hard to find a place to look. Over the edge left a sinking feeling in her stomach. Through the grate of the steps deluded her equilibrium, falsely altering her that she was in free fall. Treetops were an option, but her nerves were so entangled that she feared missing a step. Straight up, then. She looked up to the floor of the fire tower cabin and kept pace. The constant right turns, repeating white and orange floors, and spiraling fractals of metal were just as hypnotic as they were vertiginous. To avoid vomiting, Constance closed her eyes when she reached the door to the cabin. She positioned herself to only see the door when she opened them.

She did it. Inside the cabin of the watchtower, the first thing she did was find a chair. Seated, she decided to do nothing but breathe. Focus on breathing and only breathing. This was not only due to fatigue. She also knew this might be her last chance to have a solitary thought. Then it was gone.

She sat up and found east. There it was. Through a pane of hazed atmosphere, the New York City skyline nested visibly on the bluff of the horizon. It was a clear day, so the sun cast the chess set of a city as a distant mirage on a blue canvas. This was a view very few people had seen. Photos of the New York skyline were an exorbitant commodity. There are more photos of that skyline than of newborn babies. Constance's vantage point not only had the city but the wilderness before it. This harmony of virgin nature and hyperbolic industry was a rarity for the naked eye.

Constance opened her backpack and retrieved three plastic bottles with screw-on lids. She unscrewed the lids and tossed them aside. Of the four, one was empty. She sniffed each of its contents and then started pouring a concoction together into the empty bottle. Two of the contents were as dark as pitch. One thick as oil and the other as thin as ink. The third was seawater. When she believed the brew was properly leveled, Constance went back to her backpack. She cracked off a small medical lancer from a sheet of plastic. She twisted the cap off and pricked the tip of her ring finger. Applying pressure to the intrusion, Constance dripped about a thimble's amount of blood into the bottle. After shaking the contents together, she found a paintbrush in her bag. It was brand new, but the ink black slurry ruined it immediately.

Constance went to the window and painted a circle around New York City. Then, in a language older than the sun, she wrote on the outside perimeter of the ring. Before long, the window was tattooed in glyphs with only a clear view of the distant city. Constance then positioned her chair in front of the window and watched.

7

"Go fuck yourself," the gasman said as he thrust his fist in an 'up yours' motion. He then waddled away from Kaitlin's car to his brother's askew bungalow.

"Yeah, I deserve that," Rob mentioned to himself in the driver's seat accompanied by the sound of a subtle crunch. Rob was parked on an enclave of a winding hillside road. Mailboxes that were exiled from homes were staked on dirt roads just wide enough to fit a vehicle.

"And who the hell was that again," a distraught Camilla asked in the backseat.

"He was a gas station attendant that tried to save us," Kaitlin responded from the passenger seat. An additional crunch was heard after Kaitlin's sentence.

"From whom?"

"Um, from me, I suppose," Rob added.

"And who the hell are you?"

"Well, um, I'm your dad from a branch reality."

"Mom?"

"I don't know what to make of it yet, but so far, he's been… helpful," Kaitlin answered.

"From the tsunami?"

"And the converted cops," Rob added.

"Still don't know what that was."

"It'll make more sense later."

"…okay." Camilla said as she looked toward the sound of the crunch. "And what's this again?" Next to Camilla, in the backseat, sat Rudy. He folded his back legs under his thorax to create a makeshift baby seat for his more diminutive body. With his remaining legs and pincers, he was holding a bag of cheesy curls and eating them with the urgency of chamomile tea. Camilla and Rudy merely stared at each other. As Camilla did her best to maintain eye(s) contact, Rudy simply ate another cheesy curl.

"That's Rudy," Rob answered.

"And what's Rudy?"

"He's from a race of extraterrestrial arachnids that had something similar happen to their home world. We both defected from the other Earth and symbiotically share a spine."

"Share a spine?"

"Yeah."

"How do you share a spine?"

"To survive, uh, where we're from, sometimes it's helpful to have your body smithed."

"Smithed?" Kaitlin asked.

"Um, like blacksmith? Modified."

"So that's why you can…" Kaitlin motioned, pulling her chest apart.

"Yes," Rob put the car into drive.

"And that's how you…" Camilla pulled her shirt down to see a scar that used to be a terminal bullet wound, "…healed me?"

"Uh, yes," Rob said as he drove off.

"And what about Dad?" Camilla asked.

"Not me?"

"No, this reality's or some shit?"

"I called him a few times. No answer yet. I think he's still in the air, but I left him messages to meet us at the cabin," Kaitlin informed.

"And you're okay with that?"

"I'm not trying to hurt anyone, just trying to get my family to a safe place. I would have grabbed him too if he was there," Rob answered.

"But we're not your family."

"Why do you say that?"

"You're a Dad to a different Camilla. I just resemble her."

"Well, yes, but-"

"So, what happened to them?"

"Uh-"

"Are they at 'a safe place?'"

"Camilla, please," Kaitlin attempted to interrupt.

"No, I want to know. He's not doing this out of charity."

"If they were still around…I wouldn't be here," Rob mourned.

"Ah, okay, pull over," Camilla demanded.

"What? Now?" Rob asked.

"Yup, pull over and go fuck yourself."

"Hey, why? Where do you think you're going to go?" Kaitlin interjected.

"Mom, you can be hypnotized by this 'Russian Gulag' version of dad, but I'm not. Pull over," Camilla insulted as Rob acted to her whims. The car pulled over, and Camilla sprang out of the vehicle.

"Where are you- Why did you let her-" Kaitlin caught herself asking Rob as if he were her husband.

"Kat, she has a point," Rob muttered to the steering wheel. Seeing Rob's ego deflate, Kaitlin went after her daughter.

"Hey, where do you think you're going?" Kaitlin hollered at a hitchhiking Camilla. There was a swagger in her hips that concerned Kaitlin.

"Going! Where do you think I'm going!"

"Whatever!" Kaitlin swatted down a hitchhiker's thumb and waved to a passing vehicle to keep moving.

"Hey!"

"Listen, the world's falling apart, and I'm not letting you out of my sight."

"Why?"

"Cause I'm your Mother."

"Sorry, but how safe are you with literal fucking spider-man wearing dad's face."

"He saved you."

"Sure, but would I have needed saving if he wasn't around?"

Rob rolled up his window to avoid hearing their argument. He had to repeatedly remind himself to deflect their immediate criticisms. It's a preposterous situation, so their response would be equally so. Take the verbal shellacking, compartmentalize it, and pivot it off your shoulders. If experience with trauma has taught Rob anything, it's that deflecting it led to disaster, like a snowball rolling over broken glass.

He could still hear the shrieking of parental discourse. Rudy snuck into the passenger's seat. He informally clicked toward Rob. Rob looked over to Rudy, who was handing him an orange-dusted curl with his pincer.

"Thanks, man," Rob said as the two shared a stolen bag of gas station junk food. Rob turned on the radio in an attempt to drown out the remaining argument.

"-ation of the entire eastern seaboard is an undertaking beyond what the coast guard is capable of. It's been all hands on deck for every branch of the military since this morning. US troops are being withdrawn from the Middle East to aid in the catastrophe and the dispatched troops that were sent to South America are being called back to aid in-" the radio reported. Rob sighed at the news and attempted to change the station. Music was not to be heard. It may have been a different voice, but regurgitated news was the only option. "Figured," Rob groaned as he leaned back in his chair. "What else is there to talk about?"

"-suggest that the intensity of the wave is indicative of displacement, so that would mean something like a landslide of meteorite, but the wave traveling north suggests tectonic activity, much like an earthquake. Unfortunately, a seismic event like this would register on the Richter scale, and geologists can't seem to find such seismic activity. This is all conjecture, however, as most of the east coast sites have either been evacuated or taken over. Get inland now. If you are within fifty-five miles of the North American coast, get inland. If you can find shelter with friends or family, do it, but more importantly, just leave. The military is doing its best to evacuate, and if you are in dire straits, find shelter on a building rooftop. Something over eight stories minimum. New Jersey and New York City were recently devastated by the tsunami. We implore Connecticut and Rhode Island to vacate their homes and move inland."

"…I'm still compelled to dig," Rob said to Rudy with a crack in his timbre. "Fuck, man…" Rob rested his head in his hands. "What are we even doing? It's…it's too much…" The visage pried itself into Rob's amygdala. For so long, he denied entrance to the mere whisper of its name. Now, the warden of his sorrows and the harbinger of the intangible will make its existence known. The gloom boiled inside Rob's skull. Composure was no longer a word Rob could identify.

"Dad could be dead for all you know!" Camilla hollered at her mother.

"Do you not think I've thought about that! We're doing everything we can!"

"'We?' Don't throw in that stringy monst-" Camilla's argument was struck down by the sight of Rob. Forlorn by bottomless grief, Rob whimpered in the driver's seat. Rudy scurried onto his lap and did his best to console his sorrow.

Sighing at the sight, Camilla's fuming mind was doused by the brittle visage. "Ugh, I have no idea what's going on." The man that looked like her dad was fighting a private war in his mind. He did not wear it well.

—

Robert looked at his bound hands. He was handcuffed through the door grip but not to the handle. The grip was a hard plastic that was an extension of the entire door. The handle mechanism looked flimsy. Flimsy enough that he could potentially sheer it from the door, unlock it, and take his chances in the woods. Robert immediately felt humiliated after his fantasy. He would feel a similar indignity after projecting himself as a drummer for a classic rock band, but the sobering consequences of this simulation intensified that embarrassment. Instead, he looked out of the window and to his captors.

Why did the woman send Robert into catatonia? She looked as if she weighed a little more than one hundred pounds. While the man had a personality, the woman felt devoid of one. Robert could surmise an intent from the man, but the woman was a mystery. It was something beyond detachment or coldness. Absent. She was absent. Her entire presence was reminiscent of being watched from a distance. That abstract and primordial fear of being prey. She was the walking essence of that dread.

Cici and Leonard each dug their own independent hole in the ground. In a patch of clearing, they used the headlights of their stolen vehicle to see their work. They were both using their bare hands but doing their best not to soil their clothes.

"Done," Cici said, looking down at her foot-deep divot in the dirt.

"Not fair. You're tiny," Leonard added while still on his knees.

"Eh," Cici shrugged.

"Think we should turn on the radio for him? Let him hear it?" Leonard asked as he got to his feet.

Cici sneered at the sight of Robert. Making brief eye contact, Robert averted his eyes to the floor. "I'm still not sure why we can't just show them his head?"

"I mean, if you really, really, really, want to, fine. I think I saw a cooler in the back. But if you don't want the other Robert going apeshit, we need him alive."

"I can handle him."

"Sure. Me too, but he has a knack for getting away. The dude knows how to defect. He and his crafty partner-in-crime have made lives out of it. We lose any leverage, bam, he'll make a break for it, with, you know, his family."

"If it gets too arduous, he'll abandon them."

"Exactly, that too. Show them a living real Dad, they'll be conflicted, and, in turn, so will he. We show them a severed head, he'll just snag 'em and run or just run."

With the eyes a wolf might use to look at rabbits, Cici remained transfixed on Robert.

"Play your cards right, you'll get to rip off his head twice," Leonard added.

Cici nodded and looked down to her prayer hole. "It's time."

"Let's do it," Leonard responded as the two kneeled down to their respective shallow graves. With their palms in the dirt, they kept their eyes open as they buried them into the lip of their mounds. Even though they were barely human, forcing your eyes to make direct contact with the earth was an agonizing experience.

8

Every channel was news, and the news was the tsunami. Outlets had a plethora of angles to choose from due to civilian-submitted footage. Specialists commented on how close the displacement was to the shore. Since it didn't have the space to gain momentum, the flood velocity was proportionally slow. Speed, not height, was directly related to a wave's potential. Structurally, New York City skyscrapers were similar to icebergs. They ran deep into the ground. They were also porous with windows and doors. The water had somewhere to go, as opposed to added pressure. There were an estimated three million dead, but the remaining five million were evacuated onto buildings and rooftops. As soon as the initial wave hit South America, gridlock made escaping by vehicle impossible.

The sky was clear, and the sun was bright. However, a swarm of helicopters cast a sporadic nightmare on the wailing city. Every window was occupied by survivors looking down at what they survived. Forty-Second street was a river that grazed the bottoms of streetlights. Cars, buses, and debris collided with each other like rafts in a stream. As time passed, cars and trucks sank, leaving buoys of tail lights to the sound of drowning car alarms.

At the time, every screen on the planet projected images of New York. As great as the devastation was, the ensuing economic catastrophe was why the world was watching. If New York's insurance and real estate markets were in jeopardy, so was worldwide commerce. If Wall Street can endure, world banks could stabilize after a few tumultuous years. Since contingency plans were in full effect, the New York Stock Exchange would continue in Chicago. Every insurance executive was in a safe room preparing to declare bankruptcy. As of right now, claims could be paid, but if buildings began to fall, owners would be forced to default off of NYC's leverage. If that were to happen, banks, all banks, would fail.

That was why it had to be New York City.

A second crest billowed from the Atlantic. Similar to the first, it was slow, but added about two feet of flooding. Traffic lights were now submerged, and ankles were wet for people on the fourth floor.

The originator emerged off Rockaway beach. Tendrils. Coarse, black tendrils with bile-green highlights arose from the ocean. Each as thick as the Empire State Building, the tentacles lashed out as they dripped waterfalls from their endlessly serrated suction cups. It lurched out of the water. The mass didn't apply to the laws of psychics. Nothing alive could compensate for its sheer size. It stayed suspended in the air. The shadow cast engulfed Rockaway Park and the entirety of Floyd Bennet Field's one thousand acres.

Under the hulking coils of tentacles, several smooth, black arches folded onto themselves like the teeth of a blood worm. They were encased in a fleshy husk that blossomed to reveal the curves of the fangs. Each longer than any bridge, the curved obelisks extricated from their pouches and unfurled. With the absence of a mouth, the impossibility of this creature became maddening. This wasn't a head, but an extension of something still submerged. It was a hand. A tendril slathered, talon gripped, and three miles wide hand.

It came down on Brooklyn, crushing Marine Park and sinking it into the bay. It used its leverage to heave its elbow joint out of the Atlantic. The crude exoskeleton was either a jagged rock face or a mucus-stained mound of ocean-deep tentacles. The entirety of the beast then dragged itself out of the ocean. As it pivoted its weight, Brooklyn sank. Already ranked from the flooding, Brooklyn was lost to the brine.

It was like watching the Himalayas erupt with life. The entire visage was obscured by water as it became the apotheosis of a storm. A body encased by a bay's worth of seawater was now pouring down on land. It stayed belly to the earth as it acclimatized to land. After a moment of stillness, it exhaled. A wall of pressure barreled its way through the state. Buildings swayed from the onslaught of air. Then, in a display that spawned a rash of suicides, it stood.

Its trudge caused houses to fold and bridges to shear. Car alarms went off in Atlantic City, and Philadelphia could see its outline through the smoke-laden horizon. The friction of something this monumental caused eardrums to rupture. Its mere existence echoed misery, and every window shattered because of it. The survivors of this divine cleansing cried out to literal deaf ears.

Its gait resembled that of a gorilla's. Two shorter back legs and two longer front appendages attached to a hulking torso. Its face was hidden under a forest of tentacles. The beard of oceanic annihilation coiled and whipped around buildings and factories, hoisting them toward the monster's mouth.

The Empire State Building crumbled once its knuckles touched down in Manhattan. The clouds of devastation polluted the blue sky, and the sun went dim. The impossible beast sat in Brooklyn and reached over to Manhattan. One claw gripped Harlem while the other took over the East Village. Then, in a wave of unparalleled destruction, it brought the hands together. In a movement that extinguished millions of lives, the monstrosity of science raised its clutched dominion. The tentacles folded over its grasp, and the interlocking teeth of its maw opened to the abyss. The divine infinite. The avatar of entropy housed the unceremonious awe of reality. It ate.

It tilted its head back, and ocean debris fell from its crown of a skull. Horns for jewels and voids for eyes, the beast looked to its conquest. Vestigial and perforated wings opened to veil its ascendancy in darkness. Earth saw its mile-high executioner and felt it swallow its despair.

That's why it had to be New York City.

9

"-god fucking damnit," Constance heard through the layers of plastic. It was still challenging to breathe despite the perforated vents. Strands of moist plastic gripped her lips while ribbons from multiple grocery bags inched their way toward the back of her throat.

"Why not," the same shrill voice grumbled.

"She'd lose a lot of blood and die, or the holes'll get infected and she'd die, or she'd be a crazy mess and not say anything and prob'ly die, so we're doing what we're doing," a female yet deep voice answered. "Come on. One, two, three."

Constance felt her equilibrium shift, and she was on the move once again.

"Two more days."

"Shit, shut up," Constance was dropped.

"What?"

"D'you hear that?"

"Hear what?"

"I keep hearing something."

"…hear nothing now."

"I think it's only when we move. Something in the trees."

"Think he dusted Leonard?"

"Nah. He 'ad backup."

"Yeah, but it's Al's top dog."

"Still can't top Leonard."

"Never saw Leonard nix a Rhan herd."

"That can't be true."

"Someone did."

"Yeah, but a clergyman ain't gonna to-" the sounds of bodies dropping followed two concussive cracks. Silence. Constance's breath began to hurry. With her legs and hands bound, all she could do was wait to see what fate had scribbled down for her end. A steely hand gripped the top of her head. She didn't even hear the footsteps of someone approaching.

"Hold still," a muffled voice commanded. The grip didn't unravel the duct tape around Constance's neck but casually sheered it apart with one hand. "Chin up," said the voice, and Constance reciprocated. The outsider then removed the six plastic bags in one motion. Constance kept her eyes closed.

"Are you Constance?" a tattoo-less Rob asked.

"I'm…" Constance kept her eyes shut.

"I'm assuming you're Constance. She's supposed to be twenty-seven. You look twenty-seven," Rob uttered as he removed her ankle and wrist bonds. "You can open your eyes."

"I don't…" Constance attempted to navigate to the other side of her anxiety, but the sound of metal crunching ceased her in the conquest.

"That's also fine. I'm not in a rush," Rob said as he positioned her hands around a tin cylinder. His fingers felt more like twigs than skin. The same temperature as the air, it seemed as if a dying tree was handing her a can. She opened her eyes to see a shirtless Rob standing over her. She then found canned ravioli in her hands. The label was peeled off, but it wasn't dented. Even starving, it's best to avoid botulism.

"If you walk with me seven miles that way, there are four more cans just like it and a mickey of Rye," Rob declared as he pointed North. They were on a trail in a dead forest. Leafless and barren, treetops were blanketed in a mist so thick that it bled into the sky. Silent lightning slithered in the clouds, illuminating glimpses of the tendril-lathered skies. Visibility was only about seventy feet before everything vanished in fog.

"Rye?"

"Whisky."

"…really?"

"I forgot the brand, but there's a pilgrim on the label."

"Uh…" Constance took in her captives' bodies in her peripherals. She was already distraught. She didn't need to directly see a corpse. The woman's head faced the sky, but her bosom faced the dirt. The stringy male was now a blimp of swollen agony with a mug etched with torment. She looked at the torn duct tape that remained on her wrists and the makeshift stretcher she was being dragged upon. It was made of kayak ores and a tattered brown tarp. "Why?"

"We have a trek that'll last about three weeks. I'm going to make sure you're fed and safe."

"You're a clergyman?"

"Yes."

"Why are you so…civil?"

"Results yield reward, not malice."

"But why?"

"Because rye not."

Constance had to remember jokes existed. She also didn't want to hear one.

"Plus, my Apostle wants to meet you."

"No…no, I'm not going to see your apostle."

"I could drag you, if you prefer."

"I don't."

"Me neither. That'd double the time. So, we're hoofing it."

Not sure how to react, Constance nodded and looked at her ravioli. Rob must have torn the lid off with his bare hands. That was enough to tell her that it was a futile gesture to try and run. Already exhausted from a lack of nutrients, but an abundance of abuse, she didn't see the point in running. He'd just tackle her. Time was difficult to gauge under stress, but this man killed two people in less than five seconds. That was a fact. If she just conceded, he'd do what he claimed. Otherwise, he wouldn't have made the offer. She hoisted the can to her mouth and drank some pre-canned Italian food.

He was clergy. Subservient fiends to the offspring of the elder deities. Demigods look to show favor and grace their consciousness to the ubiquitous. This wiry scar-man was an enemy, but he was the best devil offered so far.

As Constance ate, Rob searched through the two bodies. One of the bodies had a satchel of jerky. Rob opened the satchel and smelled it. "Yup, not for you." He folded the satchel and attached it to a carpenter latch on his pants. "Unless you're not too good for cannibalism." He then found an aluminum canteen and did the same. He offered it to Constance. "Water." She accepted it with a craven hand. After smelling it on her own, Constance drank. Being able to wash down food with clean water almost brought her to tears; a long-dead indulgence from a less barbarous time.

"Ah ha, look-y-here," Rob simpered when he found a swiss-army knife in the back pocket of a cadaver. "I bet it has…" Rob found a spoon in its compartment. "Bingo!" The jovial expression startled Constance, but she took the spoon for the meal she'd never thought possible.

On the trail, Constance shuffled while Rob stayed a few steps to her rear. The fog was disorienting enough that Constance had to look back at Rob occasionally. The walk was mostly silent, but Rob would nod if they were on the right track or point if they were veering off course. She wondered why she stayed on the vanguard. At first, she considered it a threat. A precaution to ensure she wouldn't flee. Then, as the distance between trees grew, she gradually realized she was stooped by a sly incline. There was a steep drop to her right, and with a stumble from an embedded stone, Rob caught her. He trailed behind to always have an eye on her.

"You okay?" Rob asked.

"Yeah, I think so."

"Want to take a break?"

"Can I?"

"Yeah, of course."

"Okay," Constance reached out to find her bearings, and Rob guided her to a patch of crabgrass.

"Further we go into the Appalachian, the more rock we're going to be walking over. Saps you out faster," Rob commented as Constance sat. Rob then unlatched the canteen from his waist and handed it to her. As she grabbed it, she saw Rob's bare feet.

"You're barefoot."

"I haven't worn shoes for almost ten years."

"Do you not drink either?" Constance asked as she sipped.

"There's enough moisture in the air that my better half takes care of it."

"What's a half?"

"He's asleep right now, but he usually takes care of hydration for the both of us."

"Okay," exhausted and traumatized, Constance forwent obvious follow-up questions.

The sound of an angelic horn echoed in the distance. "Ah, a Rlim," Rob commented, staring off in its direction.

"A what?"

"A mountain eater?"

"…?"

"Big worm monster? You've never seen one?" Rob questioned a tentative Constance. She felt ashamed to be so green in a world so grey. Perplexed by how that was even possible, Rob raised an eyebrow at Constance's callowness. "Well, you're about to." Rob sat on the edge of the trail Constance couldn't even see. "It won't notice us, so don't be alarmed. Most things run away from its siren call, but if you're smaller than a greyhound bus, you shouldn't worry. Good for us, though. Almost no chance of an altercation with a Rhan or Mhit now."

As the horns drew closer, the organic nature of its frequency came into focus. It was more the echoing pulse of a whale's mating call than an orchestra of brass. Its maw showed itself in the mist. It was bewildering to Constance. It was like watching a river snake its way through the air. The fog kept it a silhouette devoid of detail, but the sheer mass of the creature was enough to cause Constance vertigo. With a serpent's body, it gently swam through the air. It was hard to capture details, but its mouth resembled that of a lamprey's; folding flesh housing a cyclonic fractal of teeth.

As it passed, trees swayed from its existence, and the earth trembled under Constance. Vestigial jointed legs dangled under the animal's carriage. They were long enough that they were lost in fog but not enough to drag across the ground.

How high are we? Constance thought.

"Always reminded me of watching train cars. You know, as a kid," Rob detailed. There was no sign of the beast's presumed tail. Like a baby and a faucet, Constance fell into a trance from the rhythm of the monster's wailing and friction. She almost forgot she was a bounty for the unspeakable.

"Annnnnd, we're here," Rob declared. It was a surprise to Constance; she had mentally prepared for a much longer trek. "You can get settled. Rest up. My eyes aren't bad, but they can only do so much at night."

"Okay," muttered Constance. With his hands, Rob dusted away the dirt to reveal an oil barrel encased in the ground. He gripped onto a latch and heaved it out of the earth with little effort.

How? With such a puny body, Constance thought as she watched Rob unlatch the lid.

"Oh yeah, I saved you a coat and a blanket in case you needed one," Rob said as he removed them from the drum. "Also found you a can of spinach, just in case. You've avoided rickets and scurvy so far, so you've been getting your D and C somehow," Rob proclaimed as he removed tin cans from a backpack. "Can't promise you these are Ravioli, but I can promise you they're Italian. Oh, and this."

Rob threw the pilgrim-painted whisky near Constance's feet. There were still materials in the barrel. Constance's fears started to augment. Now that she had a moment to think, instead of walking, she projected the reality of her future. She knew the apostles were after her, and she also knew that there were no bounds to their terror. The next thing Rob pulled from the barrel was a ziplock bag with a severed hand inside.

"Oh, shit, sorry. Probably didn't want to see that." The sight broke her mind, so Constance's body took over. She ran into the dimming fog. Rob merely stood upright and watched.

"Ugh…Rudy, could you…?" Rob sighed.

Rudy launched off of his back and pursued Constance. As the chase ensued, Rob opened his chest and prepared a cocktail for his fangs.

Constance ran blindly into the murky terrain. Shrubs made the escape a depressing slog instead of an inspired sprint. Hurdling over a large patch of downed trees, she found a standing tree for support. She just didn't realize Rob's better half was already there. At the sight of Rudy, Constance leaped away and rolled down a hill. Lost by the bludgeoning partnership of gravity and ground, a briar patch caught her.

Even though Rudy and Rob wouldn't have had trouble finding her, Constance made it easier by screeching. Her thrashing only ensnared her deeper into the bog of thorns. As she tensed and gyrated, her joints became more and more entangled. Every limb was now taken by the sharp greenery. She reached out her bloodied hand, and Rob's came to answer. Unfortunately, she saw her savior's palm retract two insect tusks and pierce the skin at the nape of her forearm. Her wailing immediately ended, and she went limp, suspended by the denticulate chaos of nature. Her eyes involuntarily went dark, and the last thing she saw was Rob reattaching a mammoth spider to his torso.

Constance would have felt refreshed if she wasn't covered in scabs. She awoke in a cocoon made out of a blanket and a jacket. As she stirred awake, she didn't know if her eyes were open. It was night. She used her hands to feel her own body. Sore beyond belief and wracked with injury, she stayed in place. She fell back to sleep after a bout of self-loathing. She did this a few times and prayed not to wake up. To her dismay, she did. Longing to have died, she hit a point where she could no longer force herself to sleep. The mists thinned. Still present but not as thick, this is the closest this world could get to a warm summer's day.

She saw Rudy. He was independent of Rob and was cracking twigs for fire kindling. The campfire was set in the oil drum, cut in half long ways, and buried into the ground. He found Constance staring at her and made his way toward her. There was little agency in his skitter. Reflective of how spiders approach prey caught in a web, Constance did her best to roll away. Her mobility was limited due to how taught she was wrapped in the blanket. The irony of how spiders wrap their prey was not absent from Constance. She hoped it would be quick as Rudy climbed atop her chest.

Keeping his hominid eyes fixed on hers, Rudy reached in several directions with his four front legs. He then retrieved a tin can and the swiss-army knife. He opened the can with two pincers and retracted the spoon for the utility knife with the other two. He offered both to Constance. Arms still constrained in fabric, Constance shuddered with wide eyes. This felt like a trick, but she couldn't discern a single purpose behind the jape. Frozen in awe, Rudy then redirected the spoon into a can of star-shaped Italian pasta. He then, with a steady spoon, fed Constance. Her eyes were still enmeshed in terror, her mouth obliged to hunger.

"I'm okay," Constance declared after a few spoons. Rudy then put the can and swiss army knife next to Constance. "Thank you," Constance breathed. The 'thank' had some enunciation behind it, but the 'you' evaporated into a breathy coo. Rudy made a gesture where his front two pincers pointed toward the sky, and he crawled off her. Was that his spider version of a thumbs-up?

Constance quietly watched Rudy as he continued to build a fire. The moisture in the air made it almost impossible to start a fire without aid. Rudy went through Rob's backpack and found a zip-lock bag of plastic BIC lighters. He took one from the pack, cracked the top off and poured the trickle of fluid on the kindling. He then used the flint from the lighting mechanism to ignite a flame. Quickly, he stacked twigs atop of it. His body wasn't as fragile to heat as human skin.

Constance eventually found her way out of the blanket. Her body creaked amid repair. Muscles sore and nerves wincing at her joints, Constance limped along to the now roaring fire. Rudy and Constance traded glances.

"Tha-thank you again," Constance muttered.

"Click click," Rudy responded.

"Are you the better half?"

"Click."

"Okay," Constance said as she walked in a figure-eight, re-engaging the mechanics of her body. She saw her briar wounds. They were practically healed.

"Oh hey, you're awake?" Rob said, walking toward the fire with a carcass over his shoulder.

"Hey."

"Ya met Rudy," Rob commented as he dropped the bipedal corpse. It was slightly smaller than a man, but its head resembled that of a wolf, and leathery wings were folded under its arms.

"Rudy? That's you?" Constance asked. Rudy made a motion that resembled a nod, but used his entire body.

"Constance," she introduced herself.

"Constance?" Rob asked.

"Yeah."

"Robert," introduced Rob. "How are you feeling?"

"Um, rickety."

"Well, you fell off a rock face."

"I feel like I should be worse, though."

"A stem-cell amino acid cocktail with thirty hours of sleep will do that?"

"I've been asleep for a day?"

"Pretty much."

"That explains this grogginess," Constance remarked as she grabbed her Rye.

"We're not moving until you can, and you can't be ready until we cook and eat this guy. So, relax and rehabilitate," Rob said as he motioned to the game he hunted that morning.

Constance nodded as she swigged back a shot of whisky. "Oh god, been a while," Constance winced.

As the meat roasted over an oil drum fire, Rob read a Harlequin novel while Rudy read 'Ethan Frome.' With half a bottle of booze left, Rob caught Constance gawking.

"I like smut," he said. "Rudy likes the driest stuff imaginable. Then again, I think it reads like fantasy for him."

"Want some?" Constance asked with an offered hooch.

"Taste buds aren't the same. It'll taste like poison."

"It is poison."

"Still, not my fancy."

"You're him, right?"

"Depends on who 'him' is."

"I haven't been here long, but I've heard the rep of a clergyman from the arachnid apostle."

"The symbiotic relationship with a seventy-pound tarantula give me away?"

"Then I'd guess you'd be 'them' and not 'him. You and the wasp woman are the two I hear the most about," Constance said.

Rob opened his mouth to respond, but ended up sighing instead, "Have you run into her? How have you not been here long, speaking of reputations?"

"What did your apostle tell you about me?"

"He doesn't tell us anything. He commands."

"Well, I'm not from here."

"I got that. How?"

"I can use gates."

"Anyone can."

"Apostles' gates."

"They don't have gates."

"How do you think they got here?"

"...I..." Rob gave up. He felt that this conversation was a betrayal.

"They don't move just across space, but time. Their language. It's like metaphysical computer code, and I know the bare, bare, bare basics of that code. In fact, I miscalculated and went backward, but I know what I did wrong. Someone from a timeline before mine taught me what they knew. It's the only way to not repeat what's been happen—"

"You're a time traveler. Like back to the future?" Rob asked.

"Yes. Exactly." Constance lied. Seeing Rob reignite interest, Constance took a cautionary approach. "You wouldn't even have to let me go. You could come with me. To a time before this happened. You can't like it here. You remember how it was before this. You must have seen friends and family die. You could see them again. You could—"

"Throw that bottle over."

Constance smirked as she did what he asked. She felt she was on the verge of brokering a deal. Rob swigged from the bottle and threw it back. His face registered as if he had drunk battery acid. He snorted and gagged after the swallow. "I'm taking you to my Apostle. You best not speak to me with such sacrilege again."

Rob did his best to keep the remainder of the excursion professional, but time did what time does.

10

Long after the incident, Constance remained seated. Her stomach wrenched from woe and she decided against moving until it slacked. She didn't know how much time had passed, but when she decided on tea, it was the same temperature as the floor. She looked to the window of the fire watch tower. Even miles away, the glass was speckled in the ruins of the city. Thin fragments of waste clouded the air. It was a sight to behold. A clear sky but an overcast land.

Constance packed, hoisting her noticeably lighter backpack over her shoulder. Her agency dissolved into a desultory lumber. She avoided demise, but was a victim of insignificance. She had eluded dystopia before, but what is a life of avoidance? Was she to do it again? To what end? To watch the next be razed asunder? Seeing her dusted Vespa at the bottom of the watchtower, Constance slumped down on the steps. She didn't want to do anything, so she didn't. Her legs would tell her when to get up.

Constance traversed through backroads. They were difficult to navigate on a Vespa, so slowing down to a crawl to overcome a pothole or a tree branch was expected. The sun was going down, but streetlights failed to illuminate. She couldn't help but think about Looney Tunes. During World War Two, several episodes would have characters scream, 'Turn Out Those Lights!' Apparently, wartime blackouts were so commonplace that Tweety Bird and Daffy Duck would holler that as a jab at the possibility of being vaporized. She couldn't imagine this modern-day society adopting such levity. Cynical internet memes, sure, but a communal joke at the expense of fear? Hard to fathom. Then again, humanity may not have enough time to nurture such flippancy.

The little vehicle couldn't maintain its speed while going uphill. Even at its lowest of gears, Constance had to pull over to avoid it from overheating. There was tranquility in her exhaustion. She was so pent up for so long that once the levee broke, her anxiety found buoyancy. What she fought against and ran from had happened, leaving no reason to fight or run. She even acknowledged the guilt that came from that tranquility. She didn't feel it. She just knew it was what she was supposed to feel.

She took her helmet off at a roadside lookout. Her vespa needed time to cool down, and she needed time to reflect. Looking to the hillside, she saw the worms of headlights snake their way around distant roads. Power was out, so houses were silhouettes to the setting sun. Star lights of campfires showed themselves to the approaching night.

Is there anyone that didn't know? Those meth addicts in that abandoned mall? Did they know? Was their position in life now the goal? They had nothing to lose and were yielding their bodies and minds to their vices. That sounds better than having a vulnerable home or an obsolete savings account.

Silence.

Not even a bird.

Constance knew she was getting close when she saw the fork in the road. There was a discarded lump of deflated balloons tied to a tree. They used to be red, but years of neglect turned them into the color of wet moss. It was a relief. These back roads were so visually rote you could realize you were lost long after you were lost. And there they were. A nest of cabins by a sand washed lake slightly bigger than a pond. Constance drove up to the faded blue house.

Built in accordance with the landscape, the first floor in the front of the house was, in carpentry reality, the second in the back. Once vibrant in tone, the steel blue had faded to that of a baby's; hunter green was now that of sea foam; and the once egg-yolk yellow now resembled its shell.

The Vespa failed to get Constance over the slight hump in the driveway. She stopped her bike, dismounted, and let it fall to the ground. *That is enough of that,* she thought.

Tossing her helmet away, she marched to her asylum while digging for the keys in her pocket.

Constance stopped when she saw her. Kaitlin was getting a bag out of the back of her car when she saw Constance approaching.

"Shit, hello" Constance greeted.

"Who are you?" Kaitlin asked with authority.

"Hi. I'm not a threat or a freak. My name is-" Constance took a step forward.

"Stop. Stay right there, right now," Kaitlin demanded.

"I know it's been a rough time, but-"

"Who are you?"

"Constance...?" Rob interrupted. He walked off the porch and marched over to her.

"Robert."

"Look at you," Rob said with the briefest of smiles.

"Me? You!" The two hugged to the confusion of Kaitlin. "How long?"

"Two days-ish. You?"

"Four decades-ish. I just didn't know that you– Oh shit!" Constance hollered at the sight of Camilla. She approached from behind the cabin with firewood in her arms. Constance created some distance between herself and Rob. She was half-turned, prepared to make a run for her bike.

"It's okay. It's okay. I did the same thing," Rob comforted.

"It's just that-"

"I know. It's startling. You're fine. We're fine."

"Shit...shit...I'm sorry. I'm sorry," Constance apologized.

"Mom, what...?" Camilla asked.

"I don't know, honey. Just roll with it." Kaitlin answered. Her using the phrase 'roll with it' made Kaitlin crave a cigarette.

—

"Look at 'em now," Leonard mentioned as he drove.

"If they were on the fence, they're over it now," Cici added as she looked out to the bedlam. Every storefront window was shattered. The people who weren't cowering were looting, and the people who weren't looting were worshiping. Sigils people couldn't translate were being graffitied on buildings. Stolen paint cans and spray paint were being handed out to the crowd. If you were further gone, scraping your hands against brick would eventually produce red paint.

"Good. Starting to feel more like home," Leonard chortled. "Must be surreal for you. Being so close and whatnot."

"Meh," Cici grunted.

"You ever see any of that shit?" Leonard asked.

"The symbols?"

"Yeah."

"No. Never," Cici answered while keeping her eyes outward.

"Man, me neither."

"You constantly hear the stories. Flashes of darkness so black they take shape."

"Always wanted to. Sounds trippy."

"But then you wake up in your kitchen, carving it into your grandmother."

"I remember finding my landlord in the shed out back. He was drinking bleach while using his scalp to paint letters on the ceiling. He was bigger than me at the time, and he always kind of scared me, so I was fucking shook. That's all the neighborhood could talk about. They even wanted to raise money to hire a specialist on the occult."

"You mean a fraud. They wanted to raise money for a fraud."

"I mean, that was really it, right? Get one of those bullshit reality shows in town for the exposure."

"When did he make landfall?"

"New York was gone three days later."

"Now, weren't their faces red."

"Getting them torn off 'ill do that. Three days after that, Janai'ngo found me."

"You were quick."

"Wife was dead. Dogs were dead. A twitchy asthmatic that weighed less than a Rottweiler in a world where there were ants the size of Rottweilers? It was an easy sell."

"How'd it feel?"

"What?"

"Weighing five Rottweilers."

"Like I wanted to redo high school. I don't think Janai rewired anything going on up here," Leonard motioned to his skull, "but I'm still riding the high of that confidence boost.

Miss my dogs, but I wouldn't trade it for nothing. How long before Mogg found you?"

"He didn't. I found him."

"Didn't know you could do that."

"You're not supposed to, but if I was going to be recruited, I wanted to be in league with the apostle others were intimidated by. The one that ate spiders and caused pestilence just by existing seemed like the one for me."

"How long that'd take?"

"About a year."

"How the fuck did you survive on your own for a year?"

Cici shrugged with dead eyes as the answer.

"Probably what Mogg liked about you. Murder moxy," Leonard added.

"Huh, I used to get croissants from that bakery," Cici remarked. The lights weren't on inside, but slivers of movement could be seen through the cracked glass. Robert pressed himself against the window of the backseat. He kept his eyes fixed on the headrest in front of him for so long that he didn't realize what was outside. This small town's main street. He'd been here. He'd gotten haircuts here. His family had been here. He looked at Cici.

"I do miss baked goods," Leonard lamented.

"They taste like acid," Cici answered.

"Now, yeah, but I miss how I used to feel about them. Nothing really replaces my memory of butter on a biscuit. A warm biscuit."

"That's just the nature of memory. Better than it really was. That's why you can't ever really go home."

"Explains my craving for Pez."

"See."

"Memory, you nasty bitch."

Using the reflection in the passenger's side mirror, Robert examined Cici's face. He then pulled back and did his best to sit in the middle of the backseat. He started to hyperventilate. He had to close his eyes to regain the rhythm of his breath.

"Cammy?" asked Robert as his eyes remained closed. Cici became motionless. "Camilla?"

The car went silent as Cici poured concrete on her resolve. Robert opened his eyes and contemplated asking again. Leonard had to consciously pry down his smile, but he basked in the tension. The sound of Robert's tongue moistening his lips forced Cici to intervene.

"That name leaves your mouth again, and so does your tongue."

11

Kaitlin scowled as she watched Constance use her mug, a wedding gift, as a receptacle for whisky. Constance felt Kaitlin's grimace and brokered a silent treaty. She poured a second mug and offered it as a mark of solidarity. With a roll of her eyes, Kaitlin accepted her attempt at peace, and the two clinked mugs.

"Ice?" Constance asked.

"No, thank you," Kaitlin replied.

"No, is there ice?"

"Oh, there's a cooler around the corner."

"Thanks," Constance made her way around the kitchen island corner and found the cooler. She opened it and grabbed a fist full of slick ice floating in the corner. "Ice?"

Kaitlin sipped her whisky, "Yeah." Constance held out a clump of dripping shards, and Kaitlin held her mug under it.

"One more time," Constance held out the mug, and the two cheered again with more apropos spirits.

Camilla was nursing a fire in a cast-iron, wood furnace. The firewood hadn't caught yet, so she continued to feed the kindling bits discarded junk mail. The laminated article for high-end furniture took a moment to ignite, and when it did, a green hue emanated in its flame. Seeing this, Camilla bridged a log over the flames. She'd been attending this for a little less than a half hour. The wood was ripe with dehydration.

Constance and Kaitlin sat at a candle-lit kitchen table behind Camilla.

"So, you know Rob?" Kaitlin asked Constance.

"Mmhm. We're both refugees, I guess, is one way you can put it."

"From a parallel universe?"

"Uh, indeed."

"Jesus Christ."

"I know," Constance took a larger swig of booze, readying for the impending conversation.

"Can I ask how?"

"How familiar are you with particle physics?"

"Consider me illiterate."

"All right, in that case, electrons...well, everything, to a degree, let's just say everything, is made of fields. Electromagnetism and all that, but particle fields react to not just the past but the future. On a quantum level, the world of subatomic mechanics, time, and reality live in the same space, working in concert with each other. Past, present, future, what is and isn't."

"So, time travel exists? Like, Back to the Future?"

"Technically, no, but the multiverse does. But instead of everyone having goatees, it's the future. What we do here won't affect the future or the past to now."

"And you and Rob are from a future parallel universe?"

"Actually, I'm from four away. He's from one."

"What?"

"I'm a part of a lineage of defectors, I guess, but instead of descendants, they're me's. Rob and Rudy helped me in more ways than one, and I gave them the means to do the same."

"This happens every time?"

Constance nods silently and walks back to the kitchen.

"Why? What is it?"

"You know what it is. People have been inadvertently writing fiction about it for a century. Hence fields influencing the past from the future. That's why we resonate with the images. Some more than others. Some people became subservient years ago, and they just didn't know what until today. We were being influenced by what has yet to happen." Constance grabbed the bottle of whisky and slinked back into her seat. "There are Gods, Kaitlin. I'm sorry to tell you that. Older than imaginable and terrible beyond reason. They feed off our existence. But not just our meat."

"That thing that attacked New York?"

"Not even a God. A priest. An intangible beast that can take a corporal form to tenderize us. And he has apostles that are just as bad. They are on their way. The actual gods are something beyond our dimensional comprehension."

"And why are they 'Gods' and not, you know, aliens?"

"Because they didn't design just us, they cultivated our entire plane of existence. How matter and energy work. For Food. We're cattle. We're farmed."

Constance and Kaitlin startled at the sound of a wooden crash. They turned to its origin; standing over a splintered log, Camilla fumed at Constance's history lesson.

"Camil-" Kaitlin chirped.

"No!" Transfixed by the revelation, Camilla stood coiled, but with nowhere to spring. Just seeing her mother brought a humiliation that raged behind her ribs. Twenty-four hours earlier, she was attempting to build a garden, now she was told she was the crop. Bolstered by unceremonious reality, emotions she couldn't regulate forced themselves into existence. She screamed into the middle space before she stormed off into the backyard.

"Camilla?" Kaitlin asked as she stood.

Constance held up a hand and shook her head. "Let her decompress for a minute."

"I-"

"Seriously, it'll do her good," Constance recommended as she poured Kaitlin another drink.

"Fuuuuushhhhick," Camilla squealed at the sight of Rudy. The vulgarity went through every stage of Camilla's discovery; shock, realization, frustration, and then acceptance. Independent of Rob, Rudy was attempting to light a fire that he had stacked in the ash of the cabin's fire pit. The pit was made of discarded wood from fires passed, so it was ripe for catching. Surrounded by cinder blocks, Rudy used dry leaves and rust-colored pine needles as tinder. There was a gentle glow and a wisp of smoke. The combination of wind and lack of digits made igniting the kindling difficult for the self-aware spider.

Seeing this, Camilla walked over and kneeled down to the impotent fire, "Here." She held an open palm, and Rudy looked into her eyes and empty hand. Registering her tear-swollen eyes, Rudy handed her the lighter.

"Thank you," Camilla said as she reached into the stack of firewood. Rudy nestled himself near her hands to block the wind.

The lighter took a few flicks, but Camilla persisted. Once lit, she held the flame under a pocket of air under a bridge of pine needles. Her fingers felt the heat faster than the kindling, but she remained vigilant. Once the needles were engulfed in flame, Rudy stacked the leaves atop, and once the foliage ignited, the two pinned wood atop the plume. The two then sank into chairs outside the cinder blocks and watched the logs nourish the fire.

A gentle reprieve set in before Camilla spoke, "So you can understand me."

Where his eyes and mandibles were devoid of expression, Rudy's head and front pincers were animated and expressive. He reminded Camilla of a muppet. Even though their eyes and mouth were in a fixed position, their body language overflowed with life. There was also enough inflection in his clicks' to ascertain the intent of Rudy's speech. Seeing a creature such as Rudy sit in an Adirondack chair brought Camilla to the perimeter of joy.

Rudy nodded.

"I'm sorry if I offended you earlier."

"Click clack clack," went Rudy, *it's okay.*

"No, it was rude. That's on me. I'm sorry."

"Click."

"So, how'd you meet Parallel Dad?" Camilla asked.

Even though she couldn't understand his language, Rudy clicked away, and she listened intently.

"I keep forgetting my actual husband is out there. I feel terrible, but it's like Rob's diminishing my concern for him," Kaitlin admitted, finishing off her whisky inside the cabin.

"It's a lot. You are doing well under the circumstances," Constance answered.

"I don't even know if he's alive. If he made it home, he should be outside of the destruction, but his plane landed in Newark. If he made a detour for breakfast or something, he'd get stuck in traffic…it's just…oh God…even now…I feel like I'm not emoting properly."

"I can't speak for your Robert, but I can tell you from the one that I know that he loves you and Camilla very much, and he's literally going to do everything he can to get back to you."

Rob slept on the top bunk of what used to be Camilla's bed in what used to be Camilla's room.

He needed to replenish his venom. Not only did he almost empty his reserves, he all but depleted his amino acid ducts to aid in healing Camilla. He avoided showing this to Camilla and Kaitlin, but he needed a copious amount of protein and fat to nourish his biology. Before he retired for a nap, Rob unwrapped a tin foil-wrapped hamstring that he had removed from the police officer's body. He hid the lump of meat in the middle of the spare tire under the trunk. Electricity may have been out, but the cabin still retained running water. Luckily for Rob, he used the shower as a cover to consume human flesh and the running water to wash away the evidence.

No one hated Rob more than himself. Innately depressed before his transformation, becoming a herald for an arachnoid Demigod to hunt heretics for entropy has ushered in new depths to his self-loathing. Nothing brought him more shame than a mirror. Every scar and tattoo was a road map to sin. Even though he wished his parallel doppelganger would arrive unscathed, he secretly yearned for him to be dead. The mere sight of himself as complete and untarnished would be disastrous to his psyche.

However, taking a shower was bliss. There was no guilt whatsoever in eating a man's leg. There was nothing better than feeling the heat run down his scalp while chewing on a much-needed meal in the dark. Not only did it feel wonderful, the man had also been attempting to kill his family. He was literally and figuratively relishing in purpose. Sleeping after a hot shower and a satisfying meal was a luxury he never thought possible, but here he was. Family saved from catastrophe, enough food and shelter. It almost felt unfair as he stirred awake.

Kaitlin stepped onto the front porch. She found two things. One was Rob. The other was that he was a step ahead of her. The loose porch board Kaitlin and Robert used to hide tobacco under was compromised. Rob was rolling a cigarette while seated in a rocking chair. He was wearing a loose long sleeve shirt, but Kaitlin caught a glimpse of the translucent membrane that revealed his spine. That meant Rudy was scurrying about. Even though Kaitlin's composure around a giant spider was building momentum, it was still unsettling.

He had already rolled a cigarette and offered it to Kaitlin. She sat down next to him in the other rocking chair. She'd done this hundreds of times with Robert. They always sat in this configuration. The tranquility of their silence was magnificent. Kaitlin reached into their tin of tobacco and rolling papers and found their matches. She lit Rob's hand-rolled cigarette before her own. The two locked eyes as Kaitlin lit Rob's cigarette. She didn't look at her match, and Rob didn't look at his hands. He nodded and leaned back into his chair. Alcohol may have greased Kaitlin's break in the silence, but Rob placing his left foot on the railing was her selling point.

"So…you're my husband from a parallel universe's future."

The versatility of Rob's response decimated Kaitlin. The sorrow in his eyes supporting the melancholy of his smile all came together with a somber shrug of his shoulders. The two then went back to their cigarettes. Robert and Kaitlin used to hold hands when they sat here. That was a long-dead romantic gesture. However, today, Kaitlin sat next to Rob.

12

Constance found a glass jar of trail mix in the cupboard. She poured a few in her hand and shoveled the mixture into her mouth. She had the right amount of inebriation to satisfy the dry assortment. She offered the mix. Kaitlin shook her head, and Constance shook the jar.

"I'm good on eleven-year-old trail mix," Kaitlin reassured.

"But if you're just handing it out," Rob mentioned.

"Here you go," Constance said as she poured Rob a handful. "They're not bad."

"Because of the craisins instead of raisins," Rob said as he ate the handful. Kaitlin caught that he knew that without looking. Rob filled that jar.

"You aged well," Rob told Constance.

"Not for my lack of not-trying."

"Woah, double negative."

"I can't believe you made it."

"The chances of us here. Insane. This is insanity," Rob admitted. The casual shorthand between the two eased Kaitlin's nerves. If their stories had any merit, the idea they could persevere brought Kaitlin a modicum of hope. "Were you early, or was I late?"

"Two hours there is thirty years here, so we're both to blame. Thank God my tattoos worked. I was afraid I sent you to an empty space where the Earth used to be."

"Can't bend time without space. Thank you for sticking to a forty-year-old plan."

"What else was I supposed to do? I hate to tell you this, but I saw Leonard and Cici. They actually tipped me off."

"I assumed. That must have wasted a lot of their Apostle's energy to get them here."

"We're climbing their most wanted list," Constance added.

"Portland?"

"Yeah. They followed me there, but I wrecked the gate when I shifted here."

"Good. So they had to drive to Burns to get to the east coast. We've got about 6 hours on them."

"Plus the traffic after he arrived. I wouldn't be surprised if they just gave up on us," Constance hoped. Rob looked at Kaitlin and then looked beyond her to see Camilla through the window.

"No, they're on their way."

"What are you thinking?"

"I can beat Leonard, if we're in the open. As long as he doesn't get me in a corner."

"And Cici?"

"Ugh…" Rob averted eye contact. "I'm not even sure if I could look at her."

"I understand."

"Plus, she's…you could throw her off the Sears Tower, and she'd just walk away."

"Willis."

"Willis?"

"Yeah."

"Who's Willis?"

"It's the Willis Tower now, not Sears."

"Oh. Okay. It's still tall, though, right?"

"Yeah, that hypothetical still works," Constance read the compounding anxiety on Rob's face. She attempted to redirect the conversation away from Cici but failed to alleviate his stress. "The gates should still work here, though."

"Good, if we can avoid walking across the bottom of the Atlantic again," Rob responded with a deflated smirk.

"We'll still have to swim."

"In December."

"We can try to wait out until spring, but I wouldn't recommend it."

"No. We'll probably have to do it tonight. Even if Leonard and Cici weren't on their way, that's Atlach's gate. He'll show up in a little less than a month."

"Who's 'we?'" asked Kaitlin.

"Pardon me," responded Rob.

"You said 'we'll have to swim.' Who's swimming?"

"Um, all of us."

"Why?"

"To escape this timeline, we'll have to traverse through a gate that's at the…bottom…of the lake."

Kaitlin stared at the two with little expression. Constance attempted to interject.

"I'll have to write some script to activate it and make sure we make landfall instead of dead space or inside a wall. You know, the Earth moves. It's more like computer code than a language, and some people call it angel speak, but we all know that-"

"And where'd we go?"

"Eh, to a separate timeline, most likely in the mid-2000s?"

"We're going to time travel?"

"Yes."

"And there'd be past versions of us there?"

"Um, yes."

"And then this would happen again anyway?"

"With time, yes."

"So…what? We grab our past selves and escape with twice as many people when this happens again…?"

"Um, Katilin, I suppose, but it's not exactly-" Rob attempted to plead.

"After we somehow integrate into a doomed society for a decade before the world collapses? Just keep doing that? Routinely hang out and know the endings to movies for a decade and watch millions of people die and run away collecting alternate family members? I guess we can play the stock market? God knows how well the iPhone does, so we can collect some cash until money no longer has any worth because of the collapse of the human race?" Kaitlin sardonically concluded.

The room went still. Rob and Constance fidgeted their eyes in every corner of the room while Kaitlin was an ice sculpture.

An unknown voice broke the silence, "Clandestine is their gaze and they have peered upon me! Your sacrilege will only nourish their transcend–" It preached from outside the cabin.

"Back the fuck off!" a muffled holler from Camilla.

Rob was the first outside, prepared to defend the facsimile of his daughter. Rudy beat him to it. Rob found Rudy climbing off the man's bloodied chest but couldn't see the man's face. The lifeless heap of a man was on his back, but his eyes faced the dirt. Rob was familiar with this maneuver. Rudy would clasp onto the assailant's forehead with his front legs and bore his back legs into the victim's clavicle. All Rudy had to do then was twist. Opponents were dead before they knew they were being attacked.

"Holy shit, wow," Camilla exclaimed to Rudy. Rudy nonchalantly skittered to Rob.

"Thank you," Rob told Rudy.

"Clack click," Rudy chirped.

"Oh, you're good. I was already up," Rob responded as Rudy assimilated back into his torso.

"Click"

"Refreshing. Needed a nap and a shower."

Constance and Kaitlin knocked on the window, and Rob waved at them to come outside.

"What happened?" Constance asked.

"Are you okay?" Kaitlin asked Camilla.

"Yeah, yeah. Rudy got 'em. After his front legs went up, shit, I didn't even see him move. Almost forgot he's a spider," Camilla answered.

"Was hoping we'd be remote enough to avoid this," Constance added.

"Who was it?" Camilla asked.

"Well…" Rob kneeled down and turned the man's head back to face him. The grit in his neck felt akin to a shopping bag full of nails. There was a pop that Rob had to muscle through in order to rearrange his head. A universal groan of disgust emanated from the group.

"Howard?" Kaitlin shuttered.

"Our neighbor," Rob declared as he stood up. He looked toward the closest cabin hidden between the wilderness. "Blood's dry. It's not his."

"His family?" Kaitlin continued to shudder. "He has two kids."

 Rob gritted his teeth at the scene in his head. If he was alone, he would skip the investigation. He knew he couldn't. They were the neighbors that lent Camilla an inner tube in the summer and brewed their own stout in the winter. It tasted like mud to Rob, but they were generous enough to gift Robert a growler. Hopefully the act would lubricate the transition for Kaitlin and Camilla. The world was dead. It's just a savage composite of familiarity. He knew what he'd find, but he still said, "I'll go check."

—

This is weird. It's not nostalgia, but it's not trauma, either. This might be a special feeling just for me. I always wondered how many unnamed emotions were waiting on deck for extraordinary circumstances. The last time I did this, I was mortified. Every step was almost a heart attack. Now, I'm almost placid. Why is that? It's concerning. I'm afraid I've been surrounded by strife for so long my brain acclimated stress to ordinary. My nerves were so wound up when I found out I was going to see Kaitlin. I didn't know what it would be like to see her again. Again? We never met until last night. It's still hard to swallow. Instincts told me to kill my way out of that police station just to avoid seeing her. I didn't feel normal again until I took care of those four reformed cops. Those instincts. They're concerning.

Huh, not that I was expecting anything else, but it looks exactly the same. Family photos with Christian paraphernalia speckled in between. Hardwood floors, a massive carpet, and throw rugs on every chair. With the addition of cast iron on the walls, this place reminded me more of a gift shop to a log flume than a home. Those last moments must have been devastating. Not only did the Father indoctrinate, but he also did so to a belief so far and away from Jesus Christ. Did they hold fast to Christ even though the father went berserk and a monster toppled New York? Maybe it was quick enough that they didn't go past confusion and shock. That's almost preferred.

The kitchen is where it must have started. There's still pots on the stove with tar-black stains surrounding the walls. Since there's nothing in them, I'm assuming they were boiling water, the stove stayed on, and the heat burned the walls. The place probably would have burned down if the electricity didn't cut out. The kitchen table wasn't overturned, but it's pressed against the wall, and the chairs are flipped. A three-piece wall hanging porcelain chicken set was shattered on the ground. It led to the basement door. Oh yeah. Christmas. There's a goofy Santa face made of yarn on the doorknob, and it makes opening the door tricky. Nothing crazy, just an extra squeeze.

I remember the feeling of walking down these steps. The odor of the old wood on their basement bar remained. It's almost a pleasure to smell it again. Melancholy, I guess. This was when I started to come to terms with reality. There wasn't a divine purpose. You couldn't control or comprehend yourself, let alone the Universe, so that meant everything. Literally, everything was out of your hands. It was humiliating. To acknowledge that, not a God, but Gods, exist? It was so sad. Not omnipresent sages that comforted their flock, but ancient unforgiving nightmares that did not give a shit about you. Looking back makes a tad bit of sense. We all pretended nature was a harmonious Eden. You drop a human randomly on the surface of this planet, chances are they'd be dead in ninety seconds. This is the same nature where Mother bears eat their cubs to survive.

Fuck, they're still there, and it's still a rough sight. Howard must have snapped before New York because they're long dead. Blue. His two kids and his wife. Their blood was completely soaked into the soil. The frigid temperature must have kept them from rotting. I can't smell them. Howard probably opened the basement window for ventilation. Smashing the floorboards with a sledgehammer would be dusty. They're facing east with an extra empty devout for Howard. The east side wall had a glass-encased jigsaw puzzle hanging from it. It must be close to a 10,000-piece puzzle. Taller than myself, it was a mural of Santa Claus holding a glass bottle of coke. I think Howard and his grandparents took years to assemble it. It's hard to recollect his story. I never really liked Howard.

I sit down on a stool at their bar. Facing the puzzle behind the bodies, I find some of his stout. Folded in a prayer position, their faces are pressed into the dirt under the floorboards. When I saw it almost nine years ago, I thought this sight would ruin me. How would I ever sleep again? Now, seeing it, I forgot Howard used a sledgehammer to secure their skulls to the ground. He used croquet steaks as nails. You wouldn't think you'd forget that, but I did. I can even reverse-engineer what he did. He did his wife first. Splintered stakes protruded out of the back of her head from failed attempts. His kids each had one. They had to be dead beforehand. They had to be. Unless he coerced one of his kids to hold the stakes, that's a depressing thought, but I can see a crazed Dad convincing his impressionable religious kid. How dare they pluck us from non-existence. His stout isn't that bad, actually.

Upstairs, I rummage through their kitchen. I'm not even sure why. We won't be able to take anything with us, and we should leave in the next few hours. I think I just don't want to go back to my alternate family. Poetic. I slaughtered my way across time, and now I'd rather be alone in a house with a slaughtered family. At least I can hear my thoughts here. Wait, what was that? The slightest of electronic beeps. Upstairs? I never went to the second floor the first time.

The beep does get louder when I stand at the bottom of the steps. It is faint, though. It was struggling to draw power. Even the sound of walking concealed it. It's in a bedroom.

Oh no.

Oh my god, I'm sorry.

In bed, connected to a portable oxygen tank and an IV, lies an elderly woman. Frail isn't the word. Her foggy and pale eyes barely register as they shiver. She could see me, but I doubt she can discern who I am. She didn't have the strength to lift her arm, let alone get the blankets off of her. The nightstand is made of prescription bottles and a glass of water. The beep was from the oxygen. It's about to run out. Her IV is empty, leaving a shriveled bag of neglect.

I lift the oxygen mask away from her. She doesn't even attempt to speak. Next to the glass of water is a small swab. I moisten it and then gloss her pruned lips with water. She rolls her lips like she was evening out chapstick. I do it a few times until she stops. How long has she been alone? I guess since Howard turned? After one last gasp of a battery-powered beep, her oxygen dies. She'll die soon, but she'll die under someone's supervision.

I turn away just in case she could see this. I open my chest and squeeze the sac closer to my neck. I then lubricate my wrist fang with the gentlest and most diluted poison I can muster. It strains my diaphragm to add this much hydration. Once primed, I pierce her IV tap and release the venom into her. I close my chest and sit at the edge of the bed. I try to tell her everything is going to be okay, but I abandon it when my voice cracks on 'everything.' I found her left arm under a sea of blankets to ensure her intravenous needle was intact. I can see the fluid enter her vein. She reaches for my hand, and I take it. I keep eye contact as long as she wants it.

She's in the family photos downstairs. If I had to guess, a grandmother on the mother's side. I hope she didn't inherit any of their suffering. I hope I didn't do that to Kaitlin or Camilla. I feel guilty. Attempting to photocopy my experience and give it to them isn't a solution. Much like how I'm failing to react here, they're failing to react everywhere. They didn't earn their trauma. They shouldn't have taken mine. Too bad I have a surplus. That's why I'm here. I hold her hand until I see her chest stop billowing. Then I keep holding it. I want to be sure. How dare they.

"So…I'm going to load my pockets with rocks, put on these knock-off Hello Kitty goggles, and swim to the bottom of the lake?" Kaitlin reiterated while looking at the kitchen table, riddled with cabin swimming gear.

"The rocks will help you commit. Trust me. It's only seven to eight feet deep, but when you feel warm, empty your pockets and swim up. It'll be disorienting, but breathe easy. You made it," Constance coaxed.

"Breathe easy after you surface, though," Camilla jabbed.

"Right."

"Yeah, fuck that."

"Camilla," Kaitlin scolded, before adding, "But, yeah, fuck that."

"Look, I understand this is stressful and bizarre, but we don't have much of a choice here," Constance reiterated.

"I'm not even sure what's happening. Rob's been making us avoid catastrophe, so I feel like we've just been on someone else's ride."

"Like, would I have been shot if he wasn't after us?" Camilla quipped.

"Twice."

"Apparently twice, but yeah, this has been a whirlwind."

"I'm just saying, a man that looks like my husband has been kidnapping us away from danger.."

"What would you prefer? To be left to your own devices? Because then you'd be dead," Constance sighed.

"No, you two just have more…direct experience-"

"That you don't want, believe me."

"We do, and don't think we're not grateful; we're just having trouble coping with something we can't wrap our heads around."

"After we take the plunge tonight, you won't have to. That's the point of this."

"Tonight?" Kaitlin asked, trading a glance with Camilla.

"Yeah," Constance shrugged.

"What about Robert?"

"When he gets back, we'll leave shortly after that."

"No, my actual husband."

"Eh, we'll wait as long as we can," Constance said, annoyance creeping into her voice.

"And how long can we wait?" Camilla chimed in.

"Waiting longer than three hours would be unwise."

"Three hours?"

"Why?" Kaitlin asked.

"People are after us—"

"Who? Why? See! This is what I'm— we're talking about. I'm not leaving my husband to elope to the past with his wiry, future twin! Jesus Christ, that's the most ludicrous shit to say out loud."

After a deep exhale, Constance collected herself. She felt it. She was on the verge of an outburst and knew she had to contain it. However, alcohol didn't exactly tighten the screws to her temper. "Kaitlin, I understand you're—"

"And you! I'm not even sure how you fit into all of this?"

"Fair, this is all fair…it's just that—"

"How do you fit in all this, again?" Camilla asked.

"Listen, if you had any idea what your father went through to get—"

"Please stop that! It might sound whimsical and fanciful on paper, but it's not. You telling me that I'm just going to have to let my present-day husband die as I run away isn't going to slide. Why would I want to live at all with that on my conscience? She'll never forgive me for it," Kaitlin said, referring to Camilla.

"Yeah, I'm not just leaving my dad here. Ain't right," Camilla double-downed.

"Oh, I sure do respect your ladies' integrity on this, but neither of you know how bad it will be."

"We know, that's our argument—"

"If you don't lose your fucking minds and kill each other, or if some other converted lunatic doesn't massacre you and bury your head in the dirt, or if the elements from a sunless sky in a South American tundra don't kill you, you'll be hunted down by an army of half-monster clergy members that will physically and mentally torture you in every brutal and perverse way possible until your psyches melt from decades of abuse, just so your soul can be drunk by a maddening legion of celestial deities older than time, undying yet begging to, cursed to exist in a vacuum of cold and spired flesh. That is where I'm from. It is torment incarnate. It is unimaginable, and that is exactly the way they want it. Now, you can keep belittling our actions with your virginal morals, or you can engage with the circumstances and be saved from a reality of endless fucking suffering. Jesus Christ!"

Camilla thought about interjecting, but the mere click of her lips as they opened set Constance spiraling.

"And at least you get a choice! At least you have the opportunity to feel guilty. I've killed for the luxury of regret in a temperature-controlled room with a full stomach and a neighbor that doesn't want to drag me by a meat hook to a pit for group 'coition!' All you assholes have to do is listen to us for less than a day, and you can't help but go and fuck that up, you ungrateful, useless twats."

Fuming from disrespect, Constance froze in place, staring at the floor. Her outburst almost thawed Kaitlin's reservations, but her second monologue solidified them. Tension filled the cabin, and Kaitlin looked for the keys to the car. When she found them on the kitchen island, her eyes went to find a weapon. With the fireplace poker in her peripherals, Kaitlin went for the keys. Silently yet sternly, she grabbed them with confidence.

Constance lunged at her and gripped her wrists.

"Don't, just don't. Camilla—" Kaitlin attempted to threaten.

"I'm going to let you go, but know you will think of and regret this moment daily," Constance uttered with the cadence of a sociopath.

"Guys," Camilla exclaimed as she looked out the window.

"As trailer-voice as you sound right now, yeah-" Kaitlin snapped her hand out of Constance's grip. "We're leaving."

"Guys," Camilla repeated.

"Very well," Constance said while ignoring Camilla.

"Guys!"

"What!" Kaitlin barked.

"There's a car out–" As Camilla attempted to alert Kaitlin and Constance, the doorknob erupted with activity. While an intruder fidgeted with the door, Constance grabbed the fireplace poker, and Kaitlin positioned her keys in her fist as a weapon.

"Ready?" Constance asked.

"Fuck it, yeah," Kaitlin responded.

"Me neither, but bring it."

The door opened by way of a key, and the soft and travel-weary Robert entered.

"Dad?" Camilla winced.

"Camilla? Oh my god," Robert whimpered.

"Holy shit, Robert?" Kaitlin uttered as she lowered her battle-ready hands.

"You're…oh my god. I thought you were–"

Before Robert could finish his sentence, an actual intruder barged in and used all of their weight to place a sublime left hook into Robert's rib cage. A bone-splintering collection of snaps permeated the air as Robert was flung through the kitchen. Like a pedestrian blindsided by a bus, Robert's body was brutally contorted against the wall. Cici stood in a fear-hushed room and icily greeted her three martyrs.

"Constance…Mother…Me."

13

Some people yearn for combat. To renounce the ego and allow primeval urges to flail. It can be infinitely intoxicating. More so than any drug. Most combatants long for that violent euphoria, but when life is on the line, that sensation is amplified. Since the celestial takeover, many men and women have reveled in that physical challenge.

Rob was not one of them; he excelled in combat only because of a disinterest in self-preservation. That didn't mean he enjoyed it. He found the fight was grating. More of an exhausting and embarrassing choir than a challenge.

Unfortunately for Rob, Leonard loved fighting. So much so, that he would forgo doors or windows and merely let his wrecking ball of a body gain access through the ceiling. The theatrics of his entrance would have found him on the first floor, but his elderly landing pad secured him on the second.

"Knock knock, pincer dick!" Leonard cackled as he dug his legs out of the mangled remains of the elderly woman and her bed. With no tactical advantage, Rob attempted to flee. Leonard gripped his ankle and hurled Rob into the bedroom wall to secure his proximity. "Hope I didn't ruin a moment. What d'you think of my skylight?" The elderly woman died before she was trampled, but the unceremonious sight shifted Rob's priorities. "Ah, I missed brawling in houses. Look at all the shit we're smashing!"

"Rudy, get to Kaitlin!" Rob hollered. Rudy was gone during Rob's command, but Leonard was already mid-stride. Rudy and Leonard were now in the bathroom.

Dust filled the air, and the debris made the whole altercation a clumsy mess. Less than thirty seconds went by, and Leonard went through two walls.

He was in heaven.

"Not this time, mother fucker!" Leonard laughed as he pinned Rob against the wall. Leonard's weight subdued Rob's two primary weapons. Leonard was engineered for combat. "Not a day goes by. I don't fantasize about this shit!" He was proportionately stronger than his already exorbitant height, the weight and the elastic nature of his crustaceous bones making him durable.

In their timeline, Leonard was one of the first to be indoctrinated by his apostle. He saw little reason to deny eyes that could see in any environment, nigh invincible anatomy, and bottomless endurance. One of the few drawbacks was his evident crustacean influence. That gave enemies an obvious foible to exploit.

"Goddamn shrimp," prodded Rob as he pressed Leonard off of him. Grimacing at the insult, Leonard unleashed his masterstroke.

Some species of mantis shrimp have a single mineralized claw. A biopolymer series of spring-loaded ligaments flex the appendage. The average striking mantis shrimp can punch underwater at a speed of fifty miles per hour. Their impact yielded three hundred and thirty pounds of force from a ten-inch-long animal that weighed an average of fifteen grams. Leonard was six foot four inches tall, five hundred and twelve pounds, not submerged in water, and had such an appendage embedded in his chest. Pinned against a wall, Rob saw Leonard's shirt explode toward him.

Even though Constance remained on guard, Kaitlin lowered hers.

"Camilla?"

"I haven't heard that name for almost a decade. Heard it twice today," Cici commented.

Camilla pressed herself against the wall and crept around her future self. Cici watched her the entire time.

"Interesting…You're backwards," Cici grumbled.

Camilla darted to her father once Cici turned back to Constance and Kaitlin.

"Camilla! My daughter, Camilla!" Kaitlin hollered.

Camilla cradled her father. Robert was breathing, but he was dazed from the chronic head trauma. "He's alive."

"Must be losing my touch," Cici growled.

"You son of a bitch. You didn't have to–" Constance uttered.

"Might want to skip that phrase in our present company."

"How the hell did you get here this quick? Gates aren't this close."

"No, but there's a gate in Washington that gets you close to an airport in North Carolina. The flight to Newark is an hour. Believe me, while you were drinking yourself stupid for thirty years, I had ten to prepare."

"What do you want? Is my bounty really worth this fucking trek?"

"No, actually. It's all been a ruse," Cici flippantly admitted. As she did, a percussive crash from Rob's fight next door echoed. "But don't tell Leonard. Not that you'll have the chance."

"That's Leonard?"

"Sounds like he found Robert."

"What the hell are you on about?"

"We're going to let that settle before we get–" Rudy dropped from the ceiling during her dastardly manifesto.

Indoors, Rob could only take so many calcified strikes from Leonard. He found himself in a third room from another shattered wall. He didn't struggle to get to his feet, but his vision was blurred. Even though the situation was dire, all Rob could think was, *thank God I got a nap in.*

He peered into the next room. It was quiet, absent of Leonard's heft. Even though Rob had decent night vision, he couldn't see in complete darkness. Couple that with the dizziness, and Leonard was practically invisible. Rob noticed that Leonard could be in four possible shrouds of darkness. He faced one, kept his retracted claws to one, and kept his venom toward one. He'd then slowly turn, hope for movement, and then strike. If he could just get outside...

The first corner he checked was the winner. As soon as he turned away, Leonard struck him. Now embedded in the broken floorboards, Rob was the unfortunate victim of Leonard's density. Leaping from his corner, Leonard came down on Rob's torso. They were now on the first floor.

"What was that crack about shrimp?" Leonard jabbed as he stayed atop Rob, pinning his left under his foot.

The clatter of their battle led a shelf to collapse onto Leonard. He paid little attention to it, but Rob caught a bottle of the home-brewed stout that was raining down. With his other hand pinned, Rob hurled the bottle into Leonard's face. The foamy liquid exploded upon impact, and the shattered glass gave Rob an opportunity. He placed his feet on Leonard's hips and pressed. Leonard hit the ceiling, and Rob met him when he came back down. With his left hand glistening in venom, Rob delivered an uppercut to Leonard's skull. With the irritant blinding Leonard, Rob grasped onto his collar and leaped out of the first-floor window. He leveraged himself against the window frame and yanked Leonard outside.

"Idiot. You had me," Rob exclaimed as he dashed away and created some distance. "Now you lost me."

Rudy fought valiantly, but it was for naught. Cici didn't even fall as Rudy gripped her skull. He turned Cici's neck to a full one hundred and eighty degrees, but she continued to struggle. Baffled that he got close enough to perform this maneuver, Rudy also bit down on her cranium to ensure victory. A twisted neck and venom-laden skull would kill almost anything. Immune to spider venom and boneless, Cici was more disgruntled by Rudy's actions than slain. Gripping onto his legs, Cici clasped onto as many as possible.

She then pried Rudy off her person and used his body as a club, battering the room. Cici violently and repeatedly found hardened corners for Rudy. The strength Cici leveraged on Rudy's body made him a weighty instrument. Lost in aggression, Cici smashed Rudy into the kitchen island until it was a shattered marble pile. She then moved to the stone of the fireplace. Rudy clicked and squealed as his body snapped under the assault. Long after he went silent, Cici committed to his end, repeatedly slamming his limp body. Camilla and Constance shied away from the carnage as Kaitlin kept her resolve.

Once she had her fill, she displayed the dripping and cracked exoskeleton of Rudy for all to see. "Two down," Cici mentioned as she tossed Rudy away. She found Kaitlin's eyes. They were not drenched in fear but disgust. The expression of a disappointed mother disavowing her offspring.

Cici was not prepared for that sight.

≈

If Leonard was built for general combat, Rob was built to combat Leonard.

In their dystopian timeline, most structures and buildings were rubble. Therefore, the majority of confrontations took place in open spaces. Rob was structurally stronger than Leonard, but he weighed a svelte eighty-nine pounds without Rudy. So, if cornered, Leonard's impact could do the most damage due to the force being directly absorbed by Rob. In the open, however, Rob was less hindered by gravity. It would hurt, yes, but the damage would be minimal as the transfer of energy would have to incorporate empty space. Rob may have been flung through the air, but he was redirecting the damage.

"Bring your spindly ass over here!" Leonard hollered. "This has been a long time coming!"

Leonard invested his aggression into his machismo. It was a smokescreen, as his once impeccable vision was compromised. Rob's poison made its way into Leonard's optic nerve, and it could take forty-eight hours for his immune system to soothe the inflammation. Where Leonard's vision was an advantage, Rob's was in vibrations. His body was covered in microscopic cilia that could detect and interact with the frequency of his surroundings. It's what made him practically silent while moving, but more importantly, he could sense movement in his surroundings. Getting Leonard into the open without a wall to divide them was paramount to Rob's potential success.

"Come on, man! Let's just finish this! Do you really want to go on the fucking run again? Snag your family and go all renegade? I don't. It's exhausting. Lot of time wasted across the board if you ask me," Leonard told the forest. It was silent as Rob readied himself in the thick. "While we bicker out here, we could be with your fucked up daughter. She's with your fake one now. So what exactly is your– FUCK!"

Leonard hollered when he heard a crack in the woods. He turned in its direction and swung wildly. To Leonard's dismay, Rob had a strong throwing arm.

Rob clung onto the distracted Leonard's back and wrapped his legs around his waist. He waited for Leonard to extract his chest claw and then secured his legs under the appendage. Unable to retract his primary weapon, Leonard ran with Rob clasped onto his back. Rob wrapped his arms around Leonard's neck and dug the fangs of his right hand into Leonard's jaw. He wanted to keep the toxins in Leonard's head, so he constricted the blood flow from his neck. The collaboration of poisoning and strangling was devastating, and Rob endured Leonard's death throttle.

Leonard rolled across the ground and attempted to find a tree to drive Rob into. There were plenty of trees, but his poison-slick eyes didn't help find them. Leonard fell to his back and, therefore, fell onto Rob. Rob waited as Leonard's appendages slowed and his infected red eyes bulged.

After Leonard was subdued, Rob rolled him off his person. Leonard gently swung at the nothing in front of him as his face swelled.

Rob watched.

"I never got satisfaction from stuff like this," Rob said as he caught his breath. "But you," he stood up and looked at his cabin. "You almost got me there."

Leonard stopped moving as the roof of the cabin they fought inside collapsed.

"It's profound how not ready I am for this."

≈

Inside, Camilla watched as Rudy's broken limbs twitched and his jaw spasmed. Rudy willed himself to stay conscious, but it was a taxing undertaking. She looked down at her father in a similar strait. His eyes opened, and he saw his daughter. "I…I…"

"Dad, you're okay. You're okay. Hang in there," Camilla assured.

Kaitlin remained standing as Constance abandoned any form of defense.

"Rudy…?" she said in a forlorn daze, but Cici placed her hand on her shoulder.

Influenced by her imposing nemesis, Constance slunk down onto the kitchen table. Cici lit an electric cigarette and offered it to the seated Constance. She took it, inhaled it, and handed it back to Cici. Kaitlin was mentally calculating how to steal the keys off the counter while somehow also getting her daughter, Rudy, and her husband into the car. Getting just herself outside seemed impossible, so adding to the fantasy was just that.

"Hey, Mom," Cici called while offering her an electric cigarette.

"What?" Kaitlin responded. As she looked at Cici, she saw that the stolen van had blocked her car in. "Well, shit."

"It'll cool your nerves."

"You tried to kill my husband."

"He'd be dead if I tried," Cici mocked after an inhale.

"Go fuck yourself," Kaitlin responded.

"Fair. You find your wife or life partner or whatever nomenclature here?" Cici asked Constance.

"I left them alone this time around," Constance responded.

"Just letting young you deal with that?"

"I'm done with it."

"Really?"

"…yes," Constance whispered in disgrace.

"After how many generations? Eight? I thought that was your blood's mission in life?"

"To what end?" Constance shrugged.

"Ah, that's a shame. A part of me endorsed your efforts. You and yourselves, you exploited a loophole in the recursive nature of time."

"We weren't doing anything new. We couldn't have been."

"The apostles seemed to differ."

Constance looked up to her would-be executioner.

"Or you wouldn't have been a priority," Cici mentioned while snuffing out her cigarette on the kitchen table.

"Remember when this tabletop was glass?" Cici asked Kaitlin. "Then we used quartz we found outside to carve our names into it?"

Camilla shuddered at the thought.

"What happened to you?" Kaitlin asked.

"That mangled husk of failure in the corner happened to us." Cici motioned to Robert.

"Not him. You?" Kaitlin asked again.

Cici smirked at her parallel mother. "I don't know if that's innate or you got it from social work, but you were never a fan of victimhood."

"We can only excuse our actions for so long."

"Yeah, where's the line there?"

"It's elastic, but murder's a start."

"Guess I'm way down the chain then, huh? Oh, here we go…" Cici said to a jostling doorknob.

Rob opened the door and limped inside. He ignored Cici's presence, but folded when he found Rudy.

"Oh no, no, no, no, no," Rob whimpered. He opened his splintered chest and knelt down to his aid. "Hey, stay with me, buddy." Rudy continued to tremble from his injuries, but glimmered a touch at the sound of Rob's voice.

"We've seen better days, haven't we?" Rob injected his friend with elixir, but as he did, Rudy gently stopped shivering.

"No buddy, no buddy, no buddy…" Rob lowered his head and nestled over his partner's body. Rudy held on to see his friend and no more. He got to know he kept Rob's family alive.

Rob made a noise. He didn't cry, nor did he scream. He had to encapsulate a lifetime of bereavement into a single breath. This was not the environment for grieving. He then gave Rudy one last hug. "But we got here," he whispered and looked at Camilla with a tear-kissed face.

That's my husband, Kaitlin thought. Selfishness and guilt ran through her body, but so did something that resembled pride.

Rob saw Robert and shuffled to his counterpart. "Cammy. It's okay. I'm going to help."

"I'm sorry…Rudy. I…I didn't…." Camilla squeaked.

"It's okay. I got him," Rob promised as Camilla stood up from her battered father. Before he kneeled, Camilla hugged Rob, and the two shared a sliver of mourning.

Embittered by the affection, Cici stepped toward her jealousy. Kaitlin hijacked Cici's vengeance. She could tear a cast-iron pan in half, but she did not have the will to face a mother fuming in discontent. Kaitlin merely shook her head in rage, and Cici forfeited to her mother's convictions.

As Camilla quietly nodded after the hug, Rob went to Robert. Robert couldn't believe what he was seeing, but the gentle timbre of Rob's voice made him seem angelic.

"Hey, my man…" Rob opened his chest again. His intestines were in shambles, but there was just enough of his cocktail. "I know this looks incriminating but stay with me on this. Looks like you're getting the last of it." He lanced Robert's side and intravenously medicated his time-divided twin. "Stay with us, okay? You've got work ahead of you." Robert kept his eyes on Rob and did his best to encourage his essence. "You got this."

Rob stood up and turned to Cici. He had to manually put his chest back in place as he approached. "It's okay," Rob told Kaitlin.

"I'm sorry," Kaitlin said.

Rob bowed to Kaitlin and then faced his flesh-and-blood daughter.

"Leonard?"

Rob shook his head.

"Eh, that was kind of the plan."

"Camilla, whatever judgment you have in store for me, I'm ready. But know…whatever you do…I also love you."

Stillness took a breath after the violence.

"Summon him," Cici demanded.

Panic struck Constance. She'd have to be involved.

"Camilla…I…I can't–"

Camilla pinched the zipper to her turtleneck. "Summon him."

14

Trypophobia is the disgust or aversion to numerous holes, organic in nature, tightly packed together. It's an inherited evolutionary signal flare to danger. Staphylococcus infections and the Sarcoptes parasite can leave porous obtrusions in the skin, and both are transmissible through physical contact. Insect colonies could also trigger a response. Species of termites, bees, and ants use clusters of tightly knit tunnels to enter or exit their nest or hive. A horde of Dorylus ants can skeletonize a one-hundred-and-sixty-pound adult in three hours. Bees and wasps kill more people in North America than any other species of animal (excluding primates).

Kaitlin suffered from such a phobia and seeing a woman with the same DNA as her daughter have honeycomb-shaped obtrusions for skin triggered that sensation. Besides her hands, feet, and head, most of Cici's skin was porous. She was a living wasp's nest, and her body was an enclosure for thousands of wasp-like insects. Boneless, the tensile integrity of Cici's perforated dermis could distribute, compress and expel energy with an efficiency not seen in hominid anatomy. The bored flesh of Cici's neck gave Kaitlin the strongest sense of repulsion. If she stared long enough, she could see movement under her tissue.

Cici dropped her turtleneck after the reveal. She wore a white tank-top undershirt, and the hexagonal pattern was visible through its thin fabric. The cell pattern went over her absent breasts and below her navel, implying her legs also housed insects.

"Don't swat at them!" Rob hollered. "Don't! Just don't move!"

The room was filled with a buzzing loud enough to drown out the motor of a lawn mower. Constance kept her hands on the table and forced her eyes closed. She kept her mind attuned to her breath. Camilla's grit was not as audacious, and she swung violently. She tried to exit, but wasps landed on every door knob and windowsill.

"Camilla! Camilla! Look at me! Look!" Kaitlin commanded. Holding her head and kneeling in the middle of the room, Camilla saw her mother swarmed by the flying monsters. She remained stoic. As they crawled across her arms and torso, Kaitlin kept an expression of determination. "They won't hurt you. Just don't move."

Camilla remained on the ground all but abandoned, trying to flee. Wasps landed on her back, and their weight was dense enough that she felt their many legs skitter. Robert was fast asleep under a blanket of barbed life.

As the group found their fortitude, so did Cici's horde. Rob, free of wasps, stood in front of his offspring foe. "Camilla, you know I can't summon him..." As Rob spoke, Cici avoided eye contact. She simply reached out with an extended two fingers and placed their tips on Rob's sternum. She elegantly repositioned her hips over her feet and redistributed her weight against the floor. "I can't summon my– Agh!"

Cici drove her fist into Rob's chest in less than a millisecond. The force of Cici's blow reverberated through her meshed anatomy. As the force ran through her body, she flexed when the energy reached the soles of her feet. This maneuver allowed Cici to absorb the opposite reaction from the initial clash, redirect it and compress the energy back into her target. Her body can successfully exploit and weaponize Newton's third law of motion. It was twice the impact of one already devastating punch.

Rob's sternum cracked from the maneuver. He immediately fell to his knees and vomited the corrosive remnants of his last meal. He couldn't breathe. His diaphragm was located on his chest, and that was currently spasming.

"Summon him," Cici calmly yet eerily demanded.

Rob found his breath. "I–"

"If you say 'I can't' once more, your flabby twin will die. Twice, the woman that resembles your wife. Three times, Constance. After that, I'll forgo their stingers and feed you to them alive. Their mandibles salivate formic acid to aid in mastication."

"I'll do it. Whatever he says, it doesn't matter because he'll do it too," Constance interjected.

"Can you say that again so he can hear it?"

"Rob, we're doing it."

"No," Rob wheezed.

"We can save at least one of us if we do this," Constance said through her teeth. She watched a wasp crawl off the back of her hand and onto the other. She felt its stringer graze the web of muscles between her index finger and thumb.

"Well then, let's go," Cici ordered.

"You don't need your ink?" Cici asked Constance.

"He's got all the ink we need," Constance responded as she motioned to Rob. Rob was in the dirt, facing the lake. He'd been digging a prayer grave with his hands. His injuries made the effort a nerve-wrenching slog. Seeing his anguish, Camilla went to his aid.

"That's his responsibility. You're better than that," Cici told Camilla.

Camilla looked to Cici and sincerely digested her comment. She looked at the broken Rob, digging his ditch. The lucidity of Cici's enunciation pricked at her psyche with a sense of camaraderie, like a captain coronating a freshman to varsity. Kaitlin moved to intervene, but Constance stopped her with a surreptitious shake of her head. Constance used the stick previously used to prod campfires to draw sigils around the perimeter of Rob's pit.

The act of just sitting up caused Rob to taste blood. Demeaned and shopworn, Rob looked to his surrogate family. Seeing Kaitlin about to make eye contact caused Rob to dart his eyes back down to the dirt.

"I'm finished," Constance announced, tossing away her stick.

"You're on," Cici said to Rob. After a long guttural inhale, Rob placed his open eyes on the lip of his grave.

It was quiet enough that Camilla and Kaitlin gradually became mortified. Even the gentle roar of wind or the babbling of the lake's shore vanished. The water became a flat pane of reflective glass, but the overcast skies funneled toward the ground. The sky crept its way to the water. When the clouds made contact, the water didn't ripple. Seemingly trading space, the fog glided into the pool as a structure emerged.

The rising, jagged stone started to take shape. It was a helmet to the inexperienced, but a crown to the world-weary. The back of its throne then revealed itself as it continued to ascend. It looked to be a monument rather than a flesh and blood creature. As wide as the lake and taller than the tree ops, a granite colossus sat upon a throne of calcified arachnids. In crude and edged armor, the faceless monolith sat above his congress.

Camilla and Kaitlin stared in awe as Cici and Constance remained composed. The hardened goliath was motionless as the water closest to the group became a reflective cape to a figure crawling from the depths of the lake. Not defying, but commanding natural law, a long-limbed bipedal beast wore water as robes and stood before Rob's service. Its gangly hands, feet, and jaw were the only things visible, but they were made of spindly cretaceous appendages cobbled together by the muck of the lake.

"Robert, my defected prodigy," the beast lavished with a smooth voice that ended with the sheen of a glass harp.

"Atlach, my sire. You grace me with your presence," Rob adorned as he stood, wincing in between the words.

"An empty greeting, but I appreciate the demure."

"Sire! I am here to barter for your favor," Cici roared.

"Is that so, little drudge of Mogg?"

"I bring you the highest bounty of the Apostles, and a traitor to your congregation," Cici exclaimed, referring to Constance and Rob.

"Is that a decaying disciple to Janai'ngo? Is that what I smell?"

"Yes," Cici answered.

"I despise that faction as much as yours. Which clergyman's rot is that?"

"Leonard's."

"Janai'ngo's most revered. How was he bested?" Atlach's avatar asked. A hush went through the group, and Rob realized it was his turn to speak.

"...I-me. That was me...we engaged each other, sire," Rob muttered, grappling with his injuries.

"How rank with pathos. Constance, is it?"

"Uh, yeah?" Constance announced.

"Your eyes have never met one such as me, have they?"

"Not this close."

"From a distance then, grazing buildings and folding treetops?"

"Once or twice."

"Yet, we all wish you clergy. Apologies for my diminutive projection. My essence is still relishing in the previous expanse. You don't originate in that or this world line, do you?"

"I misread script that sent me to yours, and then I fucked off to this one."

"Knowing our language is frowned upon, but teaching it is an unblemished sacrilege. Minds that can read our script wither, so you only teach it to yourselves. Each learning more than the last from what I surmised."

"Pretty much."

"How was it you translated our scripture?"

"I don't actually have any direct experience. Apparently, I had a wife that went mad with premonitions. A version of myself decided to write it down."

"The last seer that benefited from our forthcoming attained commerce through literature. Paltry compared to welding spacetime."

"She committed suicide."

"A worthwhile alternative to the tedium. Gallant to our gaze. Bequeathing more than trauma. You may not realize it, but your blood is a paradoxical outlier. Inadvertently astute."

"I was literally just trying to avoid shit like this."

"Aren't we all? Hence our envy and your wisdom. There are only ones of us but infinities of you. You are endless. Do you see how that is potentially troubling? Cattle seeing beyond the farm?"

"That would take...a lot of work, and I'm not entirely willing to do a lot of work."

"A small amount produced infinitely yields an infinite amount."

"I don't know why this matters. You got me. I'm at your mercy."

"I do. Luckily for me, you're in your fledgling years of rebellion. That allows room for opportunity…" The phantasm turned to Camilla. "Isn't that right, unsullied?"

"Please. Please…leave me out of this," Camilla stuttered to the warped reflection of herself in the liquid cloak.

"You have not yet bartered your person."

"And I'm not planning to."

"We'll see how today ends. What is it you wish of me? This congress is familiar," Atlatch asked Cici.

"I wish to be a part of your clergy. I brought you Constance and your traitor for sacrifice," Cici declared.

"Sacrifices are much appreciated, but Clergy yields an abundance of the reward. Trading one for another does not interest me, despite your reputation."

"You did so for him!" Cici hollered regarding Rob.

"I gained an outrider and a sacrifice in exchange for your well-being. Those were the terms granted by Robert and terms I found acceptable," Atlactch's words rang in the cackles of Kaitlin's mind. She noted that she was not outed by this supposed metaphysical Demigod. If Rob became a slave to this thing and Cici was spared, that left the sacrifice. No wonder she didn't even register, Kaitlin thought. She was strictly currency. Robert kneeled to the ground in reserved agony.

"What if I killed him right now!" Cici countered.

"You'd lose a bargaining totem, and the energy required to smith your body would not be worth the effort. I'd gain some residuals from your current form, but I'd have to siphon it to return you to human. I need your flesh turned canvas to craft you to my own image. It would be a zero-plus effort on my behalf."

Kaitlin went to Rob's aid. She attempted to help him stand but seeing the rim of his mouth laced with blood, she forfeited the effort. Kaitlin helped guide him to sit on the ground.

"But I am the clergy most feared!"

"But not the most effective. Even your dubious bargaining posture is motivated by erratic piques of emotion. You sought revenge for a fallen Mother that stands before you. She may not be the one that birthed you, but she cares the same. You had the opportunity for reconciliation. Instead, you did this to spite a Father that was scorched in a barbarous position. Did you think recreating your worst experience would heal your trauma? The theatrics are provocative but nugatory. Why would I want a clergyman that was so myopic and … hollow?" Atlatch answered.

"But your deal is much more agreeable," Atlatch stated to Kaitlin.

"What? Me?" Kaitlin said in awe.

"Your terms. They consolidate the appropriate amount of energy and add two to my flock. One of which will ease the other's transgressions. I would accept them," Atlatch commented to a perplexed and quieted group.

"Wait…" Kaitlin questioned. Cici, Constance, and Camilla clung to each fraction of silence. A deal was about to be made.

Can you hear my thoughts? Kaitlin attempted to cerebrally commune.

"Yes," Atlatch said aloud.

So yes, deal.

Atlatch's avatar yielded to gravity, and his shroud of water, mud, and insects fell. Earth crawled its way to Rob, Cici, and Kaitlin.

"What did you do?" Rob asked.

"Shit. I…I'm not sure" Kaitlin answered. "I'm sorry. I'm sorry."

Camilla watched in transcendental horror as her Mother, Rob, and her doppelgänger were sinking into the dirt. As gravity pulled from a different plane, they were thrust into the cold ground. Their bodies snapped under an invisible pressure as they sank. The monolith retreated back into the lake, expelling the clouds back into the atmosphere.

Panic struck Kaitlin. Every decision she made seemingly ended in agony, and those decisions lead her here. Her breath rushed as the ground mercilessly pulled at her. This was her fault.

"Look at me!" Rob yelled at Kaitlin. Her eyes were a compass on a magnet. Spinning in every direction, desperate for a sign of relief. The agony threaded beyond the physical. She now knew there was a soul. Regrettably, she discovered its divine existence due to its dissection. Anguish ran deeper than any nerve, and she wished to longer exist, past, present, future. Knowledge only added heat to the fire.

"Look at me!" the words finally found her ears. Kaitlin looked at Rob. "It's okay! You did it! You did the right thing! Know that! Know it now!" Rob demanded. It wasn't enough. Pressed against the ground, Rob pressed back. His joints sheered apart from his own resolve. Bones snapped, yet he would not yield in facing Kaitlin.

His mouth read pain, but his eyes read conviction. Even though his nerve endings were torn to ribbons, he remained steadfast. Rob didn't even recognize the zenith of pain burdened upon his spirit because he was preoccupied.

Kaitlin's panicked eyes met Rob's. "You saved them. They're free. That was you." Rob exclaimed.

Slick mud covered Kaitlin's ears as she sank deeper. The edges of her lips could taste the earth. Only "I lo-" exited her lips before her mouth filled with gravel. Her vision was her last shriveling sensation.

He had crossed time, slain endless monsters, and walked across an entire ocean to see Kaitlin. He wasn't going to let his own finite body stop him from letting her know, "I love you."

+1

Camilla knocked on the door. A twenty-three-year-old girl answered with moaning sounds in the background. Her eyes were exhausted, but her fresh-faced freckles were open to any commitment.

"Hey, Constance?"

"Yes, hey, come on in," Constance answered. Camilla entered a studio apartment with bookshelves taking up most of the wall space. "Please, take a seat." Constance moved the laundry away from the loveseat before she ran into the kitchen. "Can I make you some tea? I have vanilla lavender and orange rooibos."

"Sure, either sounds lovely."

"Gotcha. I think I'm in a rooibos mood."

"Sounds good," Camilla answered.

The wailing continued from a separate room, and Constance explained, "Excuse my partner. She's um…unwell… at the moment. But that's why you're here, isn't it?"

"I am."

"I…thank you for coming."

"Of course."

"It's… just… hard. We've seen specialist after specialist. I've started to jot down what she's been trying to say… you know…to see if it helps," Constance declared as she sat across from Camilla.

"Can I see?" Camilla asked.

"Certainly. Don't know what you'd get from it. I had a bunch of folks from the university look at it," Constance handed over a sketchbook of scribbled runes. Camilla looked at the glyphs.

"Ah, okay," Camilla exclaimed in the notebook. She then took a pen from her bag and drew a familiar sigil atop the notes. The wailing from the other room died down.

"Um, she's never…?" Constance questioned.

"I had a mentor. Passed on now, but a mentor nonetheless. She taught me– that's not right– she shared with me information that is older than any letter ever written. Your wife is getting glimpses of that language, information, in her dreams. I know this sounds like a scam, so I'm not going to charge you anything, ever. In fact, I'm going to pay you for your time. I want to tell you what my mentor has taught me. Not only to understand what your wife is going through, but also to speak to her in a way that she understands."

"I'm not… sure what…" the kettle started to whistle. "I'll be right back."

"Sure, take your time."

On the walk home, Camilla thought she saw someone that looked exactly like her, but backward.

Most structures over three stories were compromised since they were visible above the treetops. Not that all of Earth's new inhabitants had a penchant for demolishing man-made dwellings, but enough searched through any human nests for potential sustenance. Cities became pockmarked vistas of a new world. If buildings weren't toppled, they were perforated artifacts of decay and moss. Despite a land cast under perpetual grey, the sun's persistence tended to the more steadfast bryophytes. Dust from crumbled concrete and the moisture from lingering mist provided nutrition for hornworts and fungi. The sight of vacant cities etched by colossal handprints, shattered windows, and twisted I-beams let the remaining population know they were not welcome. This was no longer yours. The populace from the previous era could survive, but that would be the extent of it. Survival. Only the stubborn could thrive, and fragile human carcasses were anything but resilient.

Luckily for Teresa, her school didn't have a second floor. A few students wandered back to Clifftop Middle School after time eroded their safety. Each had radically different stories, but each ended the same way. Abandonment. With a supply of canned goods, clean water, and folding security gates at every entrance, Clifftop seemed like a secure place within a dangerous world. Yet, time did the same with their patience. One after another, students grew tired of cowering over canned pears and room-temperature water with a metallic aftertaste.

There were six in total, including Teresa. She couldn't help but think it was her. Was she so mousey and uninspiring that her peers would rather gamble with unimaginable torture than endure her company? What else could it have been? That had to be the only explanation. There were stockpiles of library books, nutrition, and water. There were even beds from last year's stage production of Peter Pan. She stayed to herself, kept her voice hushed, and asked for very little. If anything, the majority of her queries were to serve the needs of others.

Charisma may not have been on her side, but her intentions were pure. She always hoped people could recognize her internal voice, but now she had evidence to the contrary. She had good intentions stored within a repugnant visage of blotchy skin and slumped shoulders. The inability to express enthusiasm didn't seem harmful to Teresa, but she learned it was less tolerable than Armageddon. She was the real plague to humanity. No wonder she couldn't understand herself. How could she? She was defective. No. Worse. She was a monster.

All it took was a moment of doubt exalted by the ring leader. He was brash, articulate, and tall. With a wild mane of hair, broad shoulders, and a baritone voice fuelled by puberty, he was reminiscent of an adult. The six survivors prayed for someone who had answers. Anyone. Anything. Even an optimistic lie. He only needed a few choice words of hope peppered throughout an expletive-charged disdain for the meek status quo. There were even cheers when he used physical violence against Teresa's verbal objection.

Teresa was ashamed of her defensive maneuvers. Shoved to the ground, she remained catatonic as the group packed their backpacks with rations. She didn't raise her hand to protect her skull or curl into a more diminutive form. All she did was remove herself from herself. Feeling her bruises form, she merely waited for the world to go quiet. The security gate opening was a shill noise that rarely rang throughout the halls of Clifftop. Once it did, the shuffling of footsteps followed, and Teresa's grey world reverted to its morbid silence.

Sensation returned to Teresa's fingertips, and those fingertips found palms, and those palms found linoleum. Gradually reminding herself of her reality, Teresa sluggishly made her way back to her feet. She stood to a sight she wasn't familiar with—an open front door. There were several doors in the front of the school, but she was so accustomed to seeing it through the diamond pattern of the security gate. Ajar, due to the door limiter, nothing separated Teresa from the outside world.

It was more life than death. Moss, ferns, and vines draped every dead tree, streetlight, and abandoned car. She had to rebuild images of this perspective before the celestial incursion. It was a parking lot. Rife with activity and juvenile chatter. Now, it was the bedrock of a new ecosystem. One that did not welcome human intervention. One that rejected the existence of artificial light and packaged food. A world you simply couldn't wander into, or you'd become the screams amid the snarls. Nothing but a fading echo warning others of unseen teeth and claws.

Teresa wasn't frightened to hear her classmates being torn apart. She didn't even feel vindicated. She just felt languid, soaking in a tepid bath. The experience was a mundane conclusion to the new every day. Every one of their voices rallied but then abruptly ceased. Three were the initial prey, one tried to defend the group, and the last ran away. The ring leader was the runaway. He was the last to go, too, but the chase was brief. It was more sport than necessity, by the way it sounded.

Teresa gently closed the doors and repositioned the gate. The loss of rations was undoubtedly disheartening, but they took a few days' worth of school lunches where an entire school's worth of meals resided. Maybe an adult would be dismayed by how imperishable the food was for their children, but to a desperate twelve-year-old, it was a king's banquet of canned goods and vacuum-sealed feasts. They weren't even meals that required heat. A can opener and a pair of scissors were Teresa's culinary utensils.

The library was a wonderful way to pass the time, but the stuffy classics were decades away from Teresa's birth year. Not that she wouldn't get to them eventually, but the drab melodrama of a man falling in love with his cousin in the early twentieth century didn't exactly resonate with twenty-first-century adolescence. Besides the classics, the remaining stock was educational. Teresa liked learning about the natural world, but since the takeover, biology has been one and the same as history. That left math and advanced algebra did not do much to tickle the senses.

This is where arts and crafts flourished. With a copious amount of pens, markers, and paints housed in an endless canvas, Teresa allowed herself what her inner toddler was denied. Tearing down and storing the paper event banners for winter kindling, the cheap paint over cinder block walls could reasonably maintain ink. Storing paper for the winter was troubling, but that was an anxiety for the future. She needed to nurture her mind now if she was going to survive later.

Minutes went by in seconds, and the days vanished within those minutes. After a few months, every available space was etched in black-and-white murals. Highly detailed pen doodles on top of doodles on top of doodles smattered Teresa's stream of consciousness on the walls of Clifftop. She drew portraits of fading memories from a way of life no longer possible. Reality shows and roller coasters. Both were prospects only ever witnessed but never achieved.

Too small to ride anything with a loop, Teresa decided to design roller coasters as her own mythical serpents. Wild and impossible, they dropped, twisted, and looped over and over, bending around corners and dipping behind lockers only to return on the other side. On the spectrum of television non-reality reality, she cared little for romance, but loved the competition of stardom. Seeing regular people sing their hearts out in front of a panel of judges gave her a sense of vertigo no height could attain. She gave her favorite contestants the concert they deserved. The library held a few books on music theory and history, so the meek pharmacy technician from Sterling, Virginia, now had an entire orchestra with an ample woodwind section to properly harmonize her rendition of Celine Dion's "It's All Coming Back to Me Now."

Soon, the school evolved into a showcase art gallery. With little else stopping her, she colored in between the lines. What used to be a monochromatic temple of sea-foam green and eggshell white mutated into a menagerie of color. Markers kept the lines intact while paints breathed life into her murals. Unfortunately, outside forces halted the completion of such an artist undertaking. Several outside forces.

It wasn't unusual to hear the footsteps of giants crack through the trees or the chattering of pincers roam across the property, but they showed little interest in Clifftop. This was different. The sharp pitch of cackling bled through the walls before the front entrance glass shattered. Teresa was anything but prepared. The last person she saw was the group that abandoned her. She stopped counting the days she's been alone, but she's trimmed her fingernails eleven times since, so at least seven months. If the glass shattering didn't frighten Teresa, the violent pop of twisted metal shook her bones.

Stepping down from her step stool only produced an echo from a very human voice saying, "Didja hear that?"

Teresa froze in place, her eyes transfixed on her potential last painting. She was outlining the skirt of a violinist in lime green marker, scented in an apropos musk. A silence slithered by, and tension billowed. Teresa surmised the silence lasted six minutes but was actually four seconds.

"Go check it out," a booming voice commanded.

The sentence acted as a starting pistol as Teresa sprinted away without a destination. Unfortunately, faster footsteps followed. She hadn't had to run for almost a year, and her body wasn't eager to remember. She was plodding at best, and her lungs breathed in acid after a few strides. There wasn't much time. She was slowing down fast, so she sped up her decisions. She dashed into the cafeteria and slunk under a forest of chairs and table legs. She scurried until she found a dark nook in a shadowed area. Her breath couldn't steady as her throat tightened and her lungs burned. To compensate for her lack of athleticism, she merely held her breath.

The double doors slowly closed due to the up-to-fire-code closer mechanism. She watched it gradually give away her position as her assailant ran past them. There was a moment when he may have continued to stalk the hallways, but then the doors locked into place.

A muffled "Ah ha" burst through the halls before the doors did the same. Low to the ground, Teresa's eyes met tattered Chuck Taylor's under mud-caked jeans. As the heathen stalked the cafeteria, Teresa's lungs rebelled. The feet even approached her location, and all her throat demanded was air. She let air exit her nostrils, but it wasn't enough. Her diaphragm began to spasm. She was simultaneously breathing and suffocating.

With a life-sustaining inhale came a life-threatening assault.

The table she hid under flew away, and a greasy hand clutched a handful of her hair. She attempted to scream, but her brain was occupied with catching her breath. Even her own body abandoned her.

"Who ho! A girly!"

Her panicked breath limited her vision, but she saw that the filthy denim continued past his legs. A wide smile displayed what was left of his teeth. He smelled terrible, as if he had coated himself in rotting leftovers. Matted hair obscured his face, but wild blue eyes pierced through his mange. The only thing clean on this man was his knife. He gripped a curved hunting blade with a wooden shellacked handle.

"Yern' an endangered animal these days, girly!"

The doors opened once again, and Teresa's attacker harked to his superior. "Hey, hey, Captain! Looky here! She's skinny, but she'll do for lunch."

They were both men, but the man who entered looked like a different species. Tall and broad, he marched toward Teresa with an elegant machismo. A scar ran down his shirtless sternum, but that was his only imperfection. Barefoot and chiseled in flesh, this man reached out to his compatriot with both hands. Seeing them near each other was baffling. How was one so manicured and the other so desperate? How could they be from the same environment? The captain's hair was even trimmed.

"Whadda think? We can-"

The monster of a man gripped onto the forearm and neck of Terssa's capture. The snap of the ulna bone was loud enough to ring in Teresa's ears. The grasp of hair released, and she tumbled to the floor.

"Agh! What's you doi-" the aggressor tried to bark, but he was internally pulled apart before finishing. With a steady, bloodless yank, his shoulder was dislocated, and the vertebrae in his neck separated from his skull. It reminded Teresa of how her father used to spatchcock a Thanksgiving Turkey—snapping invisible bones within a rubbery skin carcass. The inert heap of man crumbled beside Teresa, and she was relieved to see death happen so fast. Maybe her demise would be just as quick.

"Sorry, kiddo. You alright?" The savior asked.

"Um-" Teresa's 'um' was the first combination of vowel and consonant she made for quite some time. Hearing her thin voice dashed her attempts to verbalize her state, so she merely nodded to the man.

"Here, I gotcha," he said as his hand dwarfed her own. Teresa instinctively reeled her body back as she retreated under a table. "Fair," the man's baritone voice regaled as he stood upright. He seemed impossible. Handsome and demure while only wearing grey cargo pants. He was somehow clean-shaven, while his dead counterpart was riddled with untamed hair. He was an adult. An actual adult. This was what they looked like now.

"Captain?" a third intruder asked as he opened the door to the cafeteria. This was the smallest one yet. Gaunt with greasy slicked back hair, his eyes immediately found his dead friend. "Whoa, what happened?"

"Keep on searching the space. I'll join you in a minute."

"What happened to Ted?"

"We'll put him on the spit."

"Yeah, but what happened?" Unseen organic clicks pulsated within the Captain's chest. As he shrugged, an appendage Teresa had never seen before emerged. Crustation-like, the scar down his chest revealed an embedded multi-joint claw. It gently swayed through the air and then retreated back into place. "Right...right..." said the man before exiting.

"Clifftop, huh? I think we lost to you in the basketball playoffs. Not that I played," the monster man said once they were alone. The Captain flippantly pointed to himself as his eyes returned to studying the art on the cafeteria walls: "Leonard."

He gently stalked the perimeter of the cafeteria, grazing his hand over Teresa's artwork. Teeth from a smile slivered across his face as he followed an impossible carnival ride. "I used to throw up on the teacup ride. Ever ride one of those? Anything that spun you around. Those ones that stuck you against the wall? Forget about it." He found the door to the kitchen and creaked it open to get a glimpse inside. Rations. Rations he showed no interest in. Teresa found the courage to peek her head out from under her makeshift bunker.

"There's um, uh–"

Leonard's glance stopped her sentence. Teresa swallowed the mucus slithering in the back of her throat along with her cowardice.

"There'splentyoffoodifyouneedanyfood," she blurted out in a slurry.

Leonard's teeth retreated, but his smile remained as he closed the door. "No thanks, kid. Palate's not quite the same these days." Teresa assumed it was a testament to age and not his eldritch biology. "You do all this?" Leonard asked, twirling his finger toward the walls.

"Um-" Teresa abandoned a second verbal stutter step for a more assured nod.

"All of them? By yourself?"

Teresa nodded once again despite her subconscious screaming for her to slink back under the table.

"I dig 'em. You got some chops."

"Um, uh-" Teresa couldn't remember her last compliment.

"Compelled to draw anything else? Weird stuff? Stuff you see when you close your eyes."

"Uh, like…what?"

"Eh, nothing. Knew the madness didn't take you from the first look at you."

"Oh, okay," Teresa didn't understand his reference, but it made her remember the last time she saw her mother. She was standing over her dad. In the basement. A place they only used for storage. Rarely did anyone in the family go down there, let alone two family members. Teresa thought three would be absurd, but she was willing to descend if invited. She wasn't. Her mother didn't even turn around when Teresa called down to her. And she reminded her mother that their favorite show's finale was on soon. Nothing. Teresa watched the final episode alone the next day. Whatever her mother was doing was more important than watching their favorite show. Teresa assumed it was her. It was always her.

When the power eventually went out, Teresa couldn't physically see her mother's back anymore. Not until this moment did she wonder if her mother was still there. She had eaten so many meals since then and slept so much. Could her mother still be there? Was her father still face down on the floor? She tried to imagine it. Some kind of adult magic she wasn't privy to yet. If this colossus with an extra appendage could mangle another so easily, why can't her mother still be in the basement?

"That's a good thing. Means you're like me, and that's not so bad." Leonard's declaration snapped Teresa out of her trance. Like him? She was like him? She wasn't like anybody, let alone someone so confident and magnificent. "Listen, you seem like you got a solid setup here. I had something similar."

"…really?"

"Mmhm. And I bet you saw some stuff, right? Stuff that scared ya stiff, like Ted here." Leonard motioned to the mangled body on the floor with a listless flare.

"Yes. Yeah. Yeah."

"Well, I'll give ya this; it's not easy out there. Ya gotta do some stuff to survive, and it's stuff you're not gonna like. It's vicious, so you can stay here, keep doing what you're doing, and I'll check up on ya when I'm passing through. Can't promise much, but I'll do what I can."

Whatever instincts to hide washed away from Teresa's mind. She even crawled out from under her safeguard and sat quietly on the floor. "Or you can come with me." Leonard kept his distance but kneeled down to her level. "And you'll never be scared stiff again."

Teresa knew her answer before Leonard even asked the question.

THE END

About the Author

Finding high-school physics exceedingly difficult, Jason Krawczyk decided to pursue his passion for filmmaking. After shooting numerous music videos, commercials, and shorts, Jason directed his first feature-length project, "The Briefcase." In 2015 Jason wrote and directed the Henry Rollins horror-comedy "He Never Died," which premiered at South By Southwest and is currently streaming on Netflix. The sequel, She Never Died, was released in 2020 on Amazon Prime with his new project "Sunset Superman," starring Michael Jai White being released in 20204

Along with directing, Jason Krawczyk has written, punched up, and ghostwritten several screenplays, novels, and novellas, with his first publication, "An Earth That Knows Magic," released in 2022 by Black Hare Press with "Reality Squall" scheduled for release 2024. His passion for writing led him to co-own "Little Ghosts Books" with his spouse, Chris Krawczyk, an inclusive cafe and bookstore that offers readers horror books from sterling classics, LGBTQ authors, and burgeoning indie publishers.

Jason's primary goals are honing his writing, directing, and storytelling craft while collaborating with the talented people he has met along the way.

ABOUT THE EDITOR

philip rowan (they/them) is a Queer, neurodivergent editor and writer based in Toronto, Ontario. They are currently working as an in-house editor for *Little Ghosts Books*, where they've worked on several recent projects, such as; *Demons and Death Drops: An Anthology of Queer Performance Horror, It Looks Like Dad, Roots Run Deep, Most Likely to Summon Nyhiloteph* and several upcoming projects still to be announced. As a personal fan of Jay's work, right from his very first novella, having the opportunity to work with him on this second edition printing was a true delight for philip.

ACKNOWLEDGMENTS

It's impossible to write an acknowledgment without making my husband, Chris, the centerpiece. Holy Moly, did "It Looks Like Dad" have a weird life. It was the first novella I wrote as strictly a novella. It wasn't an ambitious screenplay I later adapted, but strictly a manuscript from its inception. So, it was also one of my first forays into the submission game. It was accepted twice. One publisher wanted to bring it out in segments for a bimonthly magazine but then decided to end its print run after the COVID-19 pandemic. The second literally stopped contacting me. I have no idea if they even exist anymore.

Anyway, Chris, who reads everything I write, whether it's a screenplay, novel, short story, comic, or overly ambitious spec material, dug their heels in and opted for this to be Little Ghosts' first published novella. Then, in the whirlwind of legal research, design work, budgeting, and editing, you have in your hands (or on your screen) there is this- a testament to Chris' passion, care, and never say die perseverance. They routinely impress and inspire me, and I am lucky to just know them, let alone love them. So, thank you to Chris, anyone who supports Chris, and anyone who reads this book. I hope this was the debut Chris deserves.

Can I offer you a nice cheeto

in this trying time?

Fan Art by: Girard
Axelle, and Matt Fildey
and Rudy Plushies by
Sara McLean.
Thank you.

Printed in the USA
CPSIA information can be obtained
at www.ICGtesting.com
CBHW051629041024
15321CB00064B/3206

9 781738 909704